**Praise for
Rebecca Winters:**

'Sympathetic characters, a moderate pace and
a twist on a traditional plot all elevate this tale
into something special.'
—*RT Book Reviews* on
ACCIDENTALLY PREGNANT

'A fully fleshed-out relationship history,
sizzling chemistry and charming romance
make this a one-sit read.'
—*RT Book Reviews* on
THE BACHELOR RANGER

'SECOND-BEST WIFE by Rebecca Winters
is a rare gem with a stand-out premise,
memorable characters and an emotionally
gripping story of forbidden love.'
—*RT Book Reviews*

A BRIDE FOR THE ISLAND PRINCE

BY
REBECCA WINTERS

First published in Great Britain 2012
by Mills & Boon, an imprint of Harlequin (UK) Limited.
Harlequin (UK) Limited, Eton House, 18-24 Paradise Road, Richmond, Surrey TW9 1SR

© Rebecca Winter

ISBN: 978 0 263

Harlequin (UK) p
and recyclable pro
forests. The loggin
legal environmental regulations of the country of origin.

Printed and bound in Great Britain
by CPI Antony Rowe, Chippenham, Wiltshire

Rebecca Winters, whose family of four children has now swelled to include five beautiful grandchildren, lives in Salt Lake City, Utah, in the land of the Rocky Mountains. With canyons and high alpine meadows full of wildflowers, she never runs out of places to explore. They, plus her favourite vacation spots in Europe, often end up as backgrounds for her romance novels, because writing is her passion, along with her family and church. Rebecca loves to hear from readers. If you wish to e-mail her, please visit her website at www.cleanromances.com

Books by Rebecca Winters:

ACCIDENTALLY PREGNANT
THE NANNY AND THE CEO
HER DESERT PRINCE
HER ITALIAN SOLDIER
SNOWBOUND WITH HER HERO

CHAPTER ONE

PRINCE Alexius Kristof Rudolph Stefano Valleder Constantinides, Duke of Aurum and second in line to the throne of Hellenica, had been working in his office all morning when he heard a rap on the door. "Yes?" he called out.

"Your Highness? If I might have a word with you?"

"What is it, Hector?" The devoted assistant to the crown poked his head in the door. Hector, who'd been the right hand to Alex's father and grandfather, had been part of the palace administrative staff for over fifty years. He knew better than to disturb Alex unless it was urgent. "I'm reading through some important contracts. Can't this wait until after lunch?"

"The national head of the hospital association is here and most eager to thank you for the unprecedented help you've given them to build four new hospitals our country has needed so badly. Would it be possible for you to give him a little of your time?"

Alex didn't have to think about it. Those facilities should have been built long before now. Better health care for everyone was something he felt strongly about. "Yes. Of course. Show him to the dining room and I'll be there shortly."

"He'll be very pleased. And now, one other matter, Your Highness."

"Then come all the way in, Hector."

The substantial-looking man whose salt-and-pepper hair was thinning on top did Alex's bidding. "The queen instructed me to tell you that Princess Zoe has had another of her moments this morning." In other words, a temper tantrum.

He lifted his dark head. His four-year-old daughter meant more to him than life itself. For this reason he was alarmed by the change in her behavior that was making her more and more difficult to deal with.

Unfortunately the queen wasn't well, and Alex had to shoulder his elder brother Stasio's royal responsibilities while he was out of the country. He knew none of this was helping his daughter.

For the past four months her meltdowns had been growing worse. He'd been through three nannies in that period. At the moment Alex was without one for her. In desperation he'd turned to Queen Desma, his autocratic grandmother, who, since the death of his grandfather, King Kristof, was the titular head of Hellenica, a country made up of a cluster of islands in the Aegean and Thracian seas.

She had a soft spot for her great-granddaughter and had asked one of her personal maids, Sofia, to look after her until a new nanny could be found. What his grandmother really wanted was for Alex to take a new wife. Since by royal decree he could only marry another princess, rather than being able to choose a bride from any background, Alex had made the decision never to marry again. One arranged marriage had been enough.

Lately Zoe had been spending most of her time in the

quarters of her great-grandmother, who'd been trying in her unsubtle way to prepare Zoe for a new mother. The queen had been behind the match between Alex and his deceased wife, Teresa. Both women were from the House of Valleder.

Now, with Teresa gone, his grandmother had been negotiating with the House of Helvetia for a marriage between her grandson and the princess Genevieve, but her machinations were wasted on Alex.

"I had breakfast with her earlier this morning and she seemed all right. What happened to set her off with Sofia?"

"Not Sofia," he clarified. "But two new situations *have* arisen. If I may speak frankly."

Only two? Alex ground his teeth in worry and frustration. He'd had hopes this was a phase that would pass, but the situation was growing worse. "You always do."

"Her new American tutor, Dr. Wyman, just handed in his notice, and her Greek tutor, Kyrie Costas, is threatening to resign. As you know, the two have been at odds with each other over the proper curriculum for the princess. Dr. Wyman is out in the hall. Before he leaves the palace, he requests a brief audience with you."

Alex got to his feet. Two weeks ago he'd been forced to withdraw her from the preschool classes she went to three times a week because her teacher couldn't get her to participate. Fearing something was physically wrong with Zoe, he'd asked his personal physician to give her a thorough examination. But the doctor had found nothing wrong.

Now her English tutor had resigned? Alex's wife, who'd spent a portion of her teenage years in America, had died of a serious heart condition. Before passing away she'd made him promise Zoe would grow up to be fluent in English. He'd done everything in his power to honor her wishes, even hiring an American tutor. Alex himself made an effort to speak English with her every day.

He took a fortifying breath. "Show him in."

The forty-year-old American teacher had come highly recommended after leaving the employ of Alex's second cousin, King Alexandre Philippe of Valleder, a principality bordering the Romanche-speaking canton of Switzerland. No longer needing a tutor for his son, the king, who was best friends with Alex's brother, had recommended Dr. Wyman to come to Hellenica and teach Zoe.

"Your Highness." He bowed.

"Dr. Wyman? Hector tells me you've resigned. Is my daughter truly too difficult for you to handle any longer?"

"Lately it's a case of her running away when she sees me," he answered honestly. "It's my opinion she's frightened about something and hardly speaks at all. What comes out I don't understand. Mr. Costas says it's my method, but I disagree. Something's wrong, but I'm only a teacher."

Since Zoe's medical exam, Alex had considered calling in a child psychiatrist for a consultation. Dr. Wyman said she was frightened. Alex agreed. This behavior wasn't normal. So far he'd thought it was a case of arrested development because Zoe had been born premature. But maybe not having a mother had brought on psychological problems that hadn't been recognizable until now.

"If she were your child, what would you do?"

"Well, I think before I took her to a child psychologist, I'd find out if there's a physiological problem that is preventing her from talking as much as she should. If so, maybe that's what is frightening her."

"Where could I go for that kind of expertise?"

"The Stillman Institute in New York City. Their clinic has some of the best speech therapists in the United States. I'd take my child there for an evaluation."

"I'll look into it. Thank you for your suggestion and your help with Princess Zoe, Dr. Wyman. I appreciate your honesty. You leave the palace with my highest recommendation."

"Thank you, Your Highness. I hope you get answers soon. I'm very fond of her."

So am I.

After Dr. Wyman left, Alex checked his watch. By the time he'd had lunch with the head of the hospital association, the clinic in New York would be open. Alex would call and speak to the director.

Dottie Richards had never ridden in a helicopter before. After her jet had touched down in Athens, Greece, she was told it was just a short journey to Hellenica.

The head of the Stillman Speech Institute had picked her to handle an emergency that had arisen. Apparently there was an important little four-year-old girl who needed diagnostic testing done ASAP. A temporary visa had been issued for Dottie to leave the country without having to wait the normal time for a passport.

For security reasons, she hadn't learned the identity of the little girl until she was met at the helicopter pad in Athens by a palace spokesman named Hector. Apparently the child was Princess Zoe, the only daughter of Prince Alexius Constantinides, a widower who was acting ruler of Hellenica.

"Acting ruler, you say?"

"Yes, madame. The heir apparent to the throne, Crown Prince Stasio, is out of the country on business. When he returns, he will be marrying Princess Beatriz. Their wedding is scheduled for July the fifth. At that time the dowager queen Desma, Princess Zoe's great-grandmother, will relinquish the crown and Prince Stasio will become king of Hellenica.

"In the meantime Prince Alexius is handling the daily affairs of state. He has provided his private helicopter so you can be given a sightseeing trip to the palace, located on the biggest island, also called Hellenica."

Dottie realized this was a privilege not many people were granted. "That's very kind of him." She climbed aboard and the helicopter took off, but the second it left the ground she grew dizzy and tried to fight it off. "Could you tell me what exactly is wrong with Princess Zoe?"

"That's a subject for you to discuss with the prince himself."

Uh-oh. "Of course."

Dottie was entering a royal world where silence was the better part of discretion. No doubt that was why Hector had been chosen for this duty. She wouldn't guess the older man was the type to leave the royal household and write a book revealing the dark secrets of the centuries-old Constantinides family. Dottie admired his loyalty and would have told him so, but by then she was starting to experience motion sickness from the helicopter and was too nauseated to talk any more.

Several years earlier, Dottie had seen pictures of

the Constantinides brothers on various television news broadcasts. Both had playboy reputations, like so many royal sons. They'd been dark and attractive enough, but seen in the inside of a limo or aboard a royal yacht, it was difficult to get a real sense of their looks.

Dottie had never been anywhere near a royal and knew nothing about their world except for their exposure in the media, which didn't always reflect positively. But for an accident of birth, she could have been born a princess. Anyone could be. Royals were human beings after all. They entered the world, ate, slept, married and died like the rest of humanity. It was what they did, where they did it and how they did it that separated them from the masses.

Raised by a single aunt, now deceased, who'd never married and had been a practical thinker, Dottie's world hadn't included many fairy tales. Though there'd been moments growing up when Dottie had been curious about being a queen or a princess. Now an unprecedented opportunity had arisen for her to find out what that was like.

Dottie had seen and heard enough about royals involved in escapades and scandals to feel sorry for them. The trials of being an open target to the world had to be worse than those of a celebrity, whose popularity waxed strong for a time in the eyes of public adulation and curiosity, then waned out of sight.

A royal stayed a royal forever and was scrutinized ad nauseum. A prince or princess couldn't even be born or die without a crowd in attendance. But as Dottie had learned during an early period in her life, the trials of an ordinary human were sometimes so bad they drew unwanted attention from the public, too. Like with King

George VI of England, her own severe stuttering problem had been an agony to endure. However, to be human and a royal at the same time placed one in double jeopardy.

At the age of twenty-nine and long since free of her former speech problem, Dottie loved her anonymity. In that sense she felt compassion for the little princess she hadn't even met yet. The poor thing was already under a microscope and would remain there for all the days of life she was granted. Whether she had a speech problem or something that went deeper, word would get out.

One day when the motherless princess was old enough to understand, she'd learn the world was talking about her and would never leave her alone. If she had a physical or a noticeable psychological problem, the press would be merciless. Dottie vowed in her heart she'd do whatever possible to help the little girl, *if* it were in her power.

But at the moment the helicopter trip was playing havoc with her stomach and the lovely sightseeing trip had been wasted on her. The second they landed and she was shown to her quarters in the glistening white royal palace, she lost any food she'd eaten and went straight to bed.

It was embarrassing, but when she was green around the gills and unable to rally, nothing except a good night's sleep would help her to recover. When her business was finished here and she left the country to go back to the States, she would take a flight from Hellenica's airport to Athens before boarding a flight to New York. No more helicopter rides.

* * *

Alex eyed his ailing, widowed grandmother, whose silvery hair was still thick at eighty-five. She tired more easily these days and kept to her apartment. Alex knew she was more than ready for Stasio to come home and officially take the worries of the monarchy from her shoulders.

No one awaited Stasio's return with more eagerness than Alex. When his brother had left on the first of April, he'd promised to be home by mid-May, yet it was already the thirtieth with his wedding only five weeks away. Alex needed out of his temporary responsibilities to spend more time with Zoe. He'd built up his hopes that this speech therapist could give him definitive answers. It would be a step in the right direction; his daughter was growing unhappier with each passing day.

"Thank you for breakfast," he said in Greek. "If you two will excuse me, I have some business, but I'll be back." He kissed his petite daughter, who was playing with her roll instead of eating it. "Be good for *Yiayia.*"

Zoe nodded.

After bowing to his grandmother, he left her suite and hurried downstairs to his office in the other part of the palace. He'd wanted to meet this Mrs. Richards last evening, but Hector had told him she'd never ridden in a helicopter before and had become ill during the flight. There'd been nothing he could do but wait until this morning and wonder if her getting sick was already a bad omen.

He knew better than to ask Hector what she was like. His assistant would simply answer, "That's not for me to say, Your Highness." His tendency not to gossip was a sterling quality Alex admired, but at times it drove Stasio insane.

For years his elder brother had barked at Hector that he wasn't quite human. Alex had a theory that the reason why Hector irked Stasio was because Stasio had grown up knowing that one day he'd have to be king. Hector was a permanent reminder that Stasio's greatest duty was to his country, to marry Princess Beatriz and produce heirs to the throne.

Like the queen, who wanted more great-grandchildren for the glory of Hellenica, Alex looked forward to his brother producing some cousins for Zoe. His little girl would love a baby around. She'd asked Alex for a sister, but all he could say was that her uncle Stasi would produce a new heir to the throne before long.

After reaching his office, he scowled when he read the fax sent from Stasio, who was still in Valleder. *Sorry, little brother, but banking business will keep me here another week. Tell Yiayia I'll be home soon. Give Zoe a hug from her uncle. Hang in there. You do great work. Stasi.*

"Your Highness? May I present Mrs. Richards."

He threw his head back. Hector had come in the office without him being aware of it and was now clearing his throat. A very American-looking woman—down to the way she carried herself—had entered with him, taller than average, with her light brown hair swept up in a loose knot. Alex was so disappointed, even angered by his brother's news, he'd forgotten for a moment that Hector was on his way down. Stasio had taken advantage of their bargain.

"One month, little brother," he'd said when he'd left.

"That's all I need to carry out some lucrative banking negotiations. Philippe is helping me." But Stasio had been gone much longer and Alex wasn't happy about it. Neither was the queen, the prime minister or the archbishop, who were getting anxious to confer with him about the coronation and royal nuptials coming up soon.

Pushing his feelings aside, Alex got to his feet. "Welcome to Hellenica, Mrs. Richards."

"Thank you, Your Highness."

She gave an awkward curtsey, no doubt coached by Hector. He hated to admit she looked fresh, appealing even, as she stood there in a pale blue blouse and skirt that tied at her slender waist, drawing his attention to the feminine curves revealed above and below. He hadn't meant to stare, but his eyes seemed to have a will of their own as they took in her long, shapely legs.

Alex quickly shifted his gaze to her face and was caught off guard again by the wide, sculpted mouth and the cornflower-blue of her eyes. They reminded him of the cornflowers growing wild alongside larkspurs on Aurum Island where he normally lived.

He missed his private palace there where he conducted the mining interests for the monarchy, away from Hellenica. The big island drew the tourists in hordes, Aurum not quite so much. He shouldn't mind tourists since they were one of his country's greatest financial resources, but with his daughter in such distress, everything bothered him these days. Especially the woman standing in front of him.

A speech therapist could come in any size and shape. He just hadn't expected *this* woman, period. For one thing, she looked too young for the task ahead of her. No wonder Hector hadn't dropped a clue about her.

"I've been told you suffered on your helicopter ride. I hope you're feeling better."

"Much better, thank you. The view was spectacular."

One dark brow dipped. "What little you saw of it in your condition."

"Little is right," she acknowledged in a forthright manner. "I'm sorry your generous attempt to show me the sights in your helicopter didn't have the desired outcome." Her blunt way of speaking came as a surprise. "Will I be meeting your daughter this morning?"

"Yes." He flicked his glance to Hector. "Would you ask Sofia to bring Zoe to us?"

The older man gave a brief bow and slipped out of the office, leaving the two of them alone. Alex moved closer and invited her to sit down on the love seat. "Would you care for tea or coffee?"

"Nothing for me. I just had some tea. It's settling my stomach, but please have some yourself if you want it."

If *he* wanted it? She was more of a surprise than ever and seemed at ease, which wasn't always the case with strangers meeting him.

"My boss, Dr. Rice, told me your daughter is having trouble communicating, but he didn't give me any details. How long since your wife passed away?"

"Two years ago."

"And now Zoe is four. That means she wouldn't have any memory of her mother except what you've told her, and of course pictures. Did your wife carry Zoe full term?"

"No. She came six weeks early and was in the hospital almost a month. I feared we might lose her, but she finally rallied. I thought that could be the reason why she's been a little slower to make herself understood."

"Was her speech behind from infancy?"

"I don't really know what's normal. Not having been around children before, I had no way to compare her progress. All I know is her speech is difficult to understand. The queen and I are used to her, but over the past few months her behaviour's become so challenging, we've lost her art, English and dance teachers and three nannies. Her Greek tutor has all but given up and she's too much for the teacher to handle at her preschool."

"It's usually the caregiver who first notices if there's a problem. Would that have been your wife?"

"Yes, but a lot of the time she was ill with a bad heart and the nanny had to take over. I took charge in the evenings after my work, but I hadn't been truly alarmed about Zoe until two weeks ago when I had to withdraw her from preschool. As I told you earlier, I'd assumed that being a premature baby, she simply hadn't caught up yet."

"Has she had her normal checkup with the pediatrician?"

"Yes."

"No heart problem with her."

He shook his dark head. "I even took her to my own internist for a second opinion. Neither doctor found anything physically wrong with her, but they gave me the name of a child psychiatrist to find out if something else is going on to make her behind in her speech. Before I did that, I decided to take Dr. Wyman's advice. He recommended I take her to the Stillman Institute for a diagnosis before doing anything else."

"I see. What kind of behavior does she manifest?"

"When it comes time for her lessons lately, Zoe has tantrums and cries hysterically. All she wants to do is hide in her bed or run to her great-grandmother's suite for comfort."

"What about her appetite?"

This morning Zoe had taken only a few nibbles of her breakfast, another thing that had alarmed him. "Not what it should be."

She studied his features as if she were trying to see inside him. "You must be frantic."

Frantic? "Yes," he murmured. That was the perfect word to describe his state of mind. Mrs. Richards was very astute, but unlike everyone else in his presence except the queen and Stasio, she spoke her mind.

"Imagine your daughter feeling that same kind of emotion and then times it by a hundred."

Alex blinked. This woman's observation brought it home that she might just know what she was talking about. While he was deep in contemplation, his daughter appeared, clinging to Sofia's hand. Hector slipped in behind them.

"Zoe?" Alex said in English. "Come forward." She took a tentative step. "This is Mrs. Richards. She's come all the way from New York to see you. Can you say hello to her?"

His daughter took one look at their guest and her face crumpled in pain. He knew that look. She was ready for flight. With his stomach muscles clenched, he switched to Greek and asked her the same question. This time Zoe's response was to say she wanted her *yiayia*, then she burst into tears and ran out of the room. Sofia darted after her.

Alex called her back and started for the door, but Mrs. Richards unexpectedly said, "Let her go."

Her countermand surprised him. Except for his own

deceased father, no one had ever challenged him like that, let alone about his own daughter. It was as if their positions had been reversed and she was giving the orders. The strange irony set his teeth on edge.

"She probably assumes I'm her new nanny," she added in a gentler tone. "I don't blame her for running away. I can see she's at her wit's end. The first thing I'd like you to do is get her in to an ear, nose and throat specialist followed up by an audiologist."

He frowned, having to tamp down his temper. "As I told you a minute ago, Zoe has already been given two checkups."

"Not that kind of exam," she came back, always keeping her voice controlled. "A child or an adult with speech problems could have extra wax buildup not noticeable with a normal check-up because it's deep inside. It's not either doctor's fault. They're not specialists in this area. If there's nothing wrong with her ears and I can't help her, then your daughter needs to see a child psychiatrist to find out why she's regressing.

"For now let's find out if more wax than normal has accumulated recently. If so, it must be cleaned out to help improve her hearing. Otherwise sounds could be blocked or distorted, preventing her from mimicking them."

"Why would there be an abnormal amount of wax?"

"Does she get earaches very often?"

"A few every year."

"It's possible her ear canals are no longer draining as they should."

That made sense. His hands formed fists. Why hadn't he thought of it?

Her well-shaped brows lifted. "Not even a prince

can know everything." She'd read his mind and her comment sent his blood pressure soaring. "Will you arrange it? Sooner would be better than later because I can't get started on my testing until the procedure has been done. That child needs help in a hurry."

As if Alex didn't know... Why else had he sent for *her*?

He didn't like feeling guilty because he'd let the problem go on too long without exploring every avenue. Alex also didn't like being second-guessed or told what to do. But since it was Zoe they were talking about, he decided to let it go for now. "I'll see that a specialist fits her in today."

"Good. Let me know the results and we'll go from there." She turned to leave.

"I haven't excused you yet, Mrs. Richards."

She wheeled back around. "Forgive me, and please call me Dottie." Through the fringe of her dark, silky lashes, her innocent blue gaze eyed him frankly. "I've never worked with a parent who's a monarch. This is a new experience."

Indeed, it was. It appeared Alex was an acquired taste, something he hadn't known could happen. He wasn't a conceited man, but it begged the question whether she had an instant dislike of him.

"Monarch or not, do you always walk away from a conversation before it's over?"

"I thought it was." She stood firm. "I deal with pre-schoolers all the time and your little girl is so adorable, I'm hoping to get to the bottom of her problem right away. I'm afraid I'm too focused on my job. Your Highness," she tacked on, as if she weren't sure whether to say it or not.

She was different from anyone he'd ever met. Not rude exactly, yet definitely the opposite of obsequious. He didn't know what to think of her. But just now she'd sounded sincere enough where his daughter was concerned. Alex needed to take the advice his mother had given him as a boy. Never react on a first impression or you could live to regret it.

"I'm glad you're focused," he said and meant it. "She's the light of my life."

The briefest glint of pain entered her eyes. "You're a lucky man to have her, even if you *are* a prince."

His brows furrowed. "Even if I'm a prince?"

She shook her head. "I'm sorry. I meant— Well, I meant that one assumes a prince has been given everything in life and is very lucky. But to be the father of a darling daughter, too, makes you that much luckier."

Though she smiled, he heard a sadness in her words. Long after he'd excused her and had arranged for the doctor's appointment, the shadow he'd seen in those deep blue eyes stayed with him.

CHAPTER TWO

DOTTIE stayed in her room for part of the day, fussing and fuming over a situation she could do little about. *I haven't excused you yet, Mrs. Richards.*

The mild rebuke had fallen from the lips of a prince who was outrageously handsome. Tall and built like the statue of a Greek god, he possessed the inky-black hair and eyes of his Hellenican ancestry. Everything—his chiseled jaw, his strong male features—set him apart from other men.

Even if he weren't royal, he looked like any woman's idea of a prince. He'd stood there in front of his country's flag, effortlessly masculine and regal in a silky blue shirt and white trousers that molded to his powerful thighs.

He'd smelled good, too. Dottie noticed things like that and wished she hadn't because it reminded her that beneath the royal mantle, he was human.

Already she feared she might not be the right person for this job. Dr. Rice, the head of her department at the Stillman clinic, had said he'd handpicked her for this assignment because of her own personal experiences that gave her more understanding. Fine, but in order to give herself time to get used to the idea, she should have been told she was coming to a royal household before she boarded the jet in New York.

The atmosphere here was different from anything Dottie had known and she needed time to adjust. There was so much to deal with—the stiffness, the protocol, the maids and nannies, the teachers, the tutors, a prince for a father who'd been forced to obey a rigid schedule his whole life, a princess without a mother....

A normal child would have run into the room and hugged her daddy without thinking about it, but royal etiquette had held Zoe back from doing what came naturally. She'd appeared in the doorway and stood at attention like a good soldier.

The whole thing had to be too much for a little girl who just wanted to be a little girl. In the end she'd broken those rules and had taken off down the hall, her dark brown curls bouncing. Despite his calling her name, she'd kept going. The precious child couldn't handle any more.

Dottie's heart ached for Zoe who'd ignored her father's wishes and had run out of his office with tears flowing from those golden-brown eyes. She must have gotten her coloring from her mother, who'd probably been petite. His daughter had inherited her beauty and olive skin from her father, no doubt from her mother, too.

The vague images Dottie had retained of him and his brother through the media had been taken when they were much younger, playboy princes setting hearts afire throughout Europe. In the intervening years, Zoe's father had become a married man who'd lost his wife too soon in life. Tragic for him, and more tragic for a child to lose a parent. Unfortunately it had happened.

Dottie was the enemy of the moment where Zoe was concerned, and she'd would have to be careful how she approached her to do the testing. Soon enough she would discover how much of Zoe's problem was emotional or physical. Probably both.

With a deep sigh she ate the lunch a maid had brought her on a tray. Later another maid offered to unpack for her, but Dottie thanked her before dismissing her. She could do it herself. In fact she didn't want to get completely unpacked in case she'd be leaving the palace right away. If the little princess had a problem outside of Dottie's expertise, then Dottie would soon be flown back to New York from the island.

At five o'clock the phone rang at the side of her queen-size bed. It was Hector. The prince wished to speak to her in his office. He was sending a maid to escort her. It was on the tip of Dottie's tongue to tell him she didn't need help finding the prince's inner sanctum, but she had to remember that when in Rome… Already she'd made a bad impression. It wouldn't do to alienate him further, not when he was so anxious about his daughter.

She thanked Hector and freshened up. In a minute, one of the maids arrived and accompanied her down a different staircase outside her private guest suite to the main floor. The prince was waiting for her.

Out of deference to him, she waited until he spoke first. He stood there with his hands on his hips. By the aura of energy he was giving out with those jet-black eyes playing over her, she sensed he had something of significance to tell her.

"Sit down, please."

She did his bidding, anxious to hear about the result of the examination.

"Once we could get Zoe to cooperate, the doctor found an inordinate amount of wax adhering to her eardrums from residual fluid. She hated every second of it, but after they were cleaned out, she actually smiled when he asked her if she could hear better. The audiologist did tests afterwards and said her hearing is fine."

"Oh, that's wonderful news!" Dottie cried out happily.

"Yes. On the way back to the palace, I could tell she did understand more words being spoken to her. There was understanding in her eyes."

Beneath that formal reserve of his, she knew he was relieved for that much good news. A prince could move mountains and that's what he'd done today by getting her into an ear specialist so fast. In fact, he'd made it possible for Dottie to come to Hellenica instead of the other way around. What greater proof that the man loved his daughter?

"This is an excellent start, Your Highness."

"When do you want to begin testing her?"

"Tomorrow morning. She needs to have a good night's sleep first. After what she's been through today, she doesn't need any more trauma."

"Agreed." She heard a wealth of emotion in that one word. Dottie could imagine the struggle his daughter had put up. "Where would you like to test her?"

Since the prince was still standing, Dottie got to her feet to be on par with him, but she still needed to look up. "If you asked her where her favorite place is to play, what would she tell you?"

After a moment he said, "The patio off my bedroom."

That didn't surprise Dottie. His little girl wanted to be near him without anyone else around. "Does she play there often?"

She heard his sharp intake of breath. "No. It's not allowed unless I'm there, too." Of course not. "My work normally goes past her bedtime."

"And mornings?"

"While we've been at the palace, I've always had breakfast with her in the queen's suite. Zoe's the most comfortable there."

"I'm talking before breakfast."

"That's when I work out and she takes a swimming lesson."

Dottie fought to remain quiet, but her impulse was to cry out in dismay over the strict regimen. "So what times does she get to play with you on your patio?"

He pursed his lips. "Sunday afternoons after chapel and lunch. Why all these questions?"

She needed to be careful she didn't offend him again. "I'm trying to get a sense of her day and her relationship with you. When is her Greek lesson?"

"Before her dinner."

"You don't eat dinner with her, then?"

"No."

Oh. Poor Zoe. "You say she was attending a preschool until two weeks ago?"

"Yes. The sessions went in two-hour segments, three times a week. Monday, Wednesday and Friday. But lately I haven't insisted for the obvious reasons."

"When does she play with friends?"

"You mean outside her school?"

"Yes. Does she have friends here at the palace?"

"No, but we normally live on Aurum where she has several."

"I see. Thank you for giving me that information. Would it be all right with you if I test her out on your patio? I believe she'll be more responsive in a place where she's truly happy and at ease. If you're there, too, it will make her more comfortable. But with your full schedule I don't suppose that's poss—"

"I'll make time for it," he declared, cutting her off.

No matter how she said things, she seemed to be in the wrong. It wasn't her intention to push his buttons, but she was doing a good job of it anyway. "That would be ideal. It's important I watch her interaction with you. Before you come, I'd like to set up out there with a few things I've brought."

His brows lifted. "How much time do you need?"

"A few minutes."

He nodded. "I'll send a maid to escort you at eight. Zoe and I will join you at eight-twenty. Does that meet with your approval?"

Eight-twenty? Not eight-twenty-one? *Stop it, Dottie. You're in a different world now.* "Only if it meets with yours, Your Highness."

This close to him, she could see a tiny nerve throbbing at the corner of his compelling mouth. His lips had grown taut. "If I haven't made it clear before, let me say this again. My daughter is my life. That makes her my top priority." She believed him.

"I know," Dottie murmured. "While I'm here, she's mine, too."

A long silence ensued before he stepped away. "I've instructed Hector to make certain you're comfortable while you're here. Your dinner can be served in the small guest dining room on the second floor, or he'll have it brought to your room. Whatever you prefer. Anything you want or need, you have only to pick up the phone and ask him and he'll see to it."

"Thank you. He's been so perfect, I can hardly believe he's real."

"My brother and I have been saying the same thing about him for years." The first glimmer of an unexpected smile reached his black eyes. He did have his human moments. The proof of it set off waves of sensation through her body she hadn't expected or wanted to feel.

"If you'll eat your eggs, I have a surprise for you." Zoe jerked her head around and eyed Alex in excitement. "I'm going to spend time with you this morning and thought we'd play out on my patio. That's why I told Sofia to let you wear pants."

She made a sound of delight and promptly took several bites. The queen sent him a private glance that said she hoped this testing session with the new speech therapist wasn't going to be a waste of time. Alex hoped not, too. No one wanted constructive feedback more than he did.

After Zoe finished off her juice, she wiggled down from the chair and started to dart away. Alex called her back. "You must ask to be excused."

She turned to her grandmother. "Can I go with daddy, *Yiayia*?"

The queen nodded. "Have a good time."

Alex groaned in silence, remembering the way his daughter had flown out of his office yesterday after one look at Dottie.

Zoe slipped her hand into his and they left for his suite. She skipped along part of the way. When he saw how thrilled she was to be with him, he found himself even more put out with Stasio.

As soon as his brother got back from Vallader, Alex planned to take more time off to be with his daughter. While he'd had to be here at the palace doing his brother's work plus his own, he'd hardly had a minute to spend time with her. Maybe they'd go on a mini vacation together.

The curtains to the patio had been opened. Zoe ran through the bedroom ahead of him, then suddenly stopped at the sight of the woman sitting on the patio tiles in jeans and a pale orange, short-sleeved cotton top.

"Hi, Zoe," she spoke in English with a smile. Dottie had put on sneakers and her hair was loose in a kind of disheveled bob that revealed the light honey tones among the darker swaths. "Do you think your daddy can catch this?" She threw a Ping-Pong ball at him.

When he caught it with his right hand, Zoe cried out in surprise. He threw it back to Dottie who caught it in her left. Their first volley of the day. For no particular reason his pulse rate picked up at the thought of what else awaited him in her presence.

"Good catch. Come on, Daddy." Her dancing blue gaze shot to his. "You and Zoe sit down and spread your legs apart like this and we'll roll some balls to each other." She pulled a larger multicolored plastic ball from a big bag and opened those long, fabulous legs of hers.

Alex could tell his daughter was so shocked by what was going on, she forgot to be scared and sat down to imitate Dottie once he'd complied. Dottie rolled the ball to Zoe, who rolled it back to her. Then it was his turn. They went in a round, drawing Zoe in. Pretty soon their guest pulled out a rubber ball and rolled it to his daughter right after she'd sent her the plastic ball.

Zoe laughed as she hurried to keep both balls going. His clever little girl used her right and left hand at the same time and sent one ball to Dottie and one to him. "Good thinking!" she praised her. "Shall we try three balls?"

"Yes," his daughter said excitedly. Their guest produced the Ping-Pong ball and fired all three balls at both of them, one after the other, until Zoe was giggling hysterically.

"You're so good at this, I think we'll try something else. Shall we see who's better at jumping?" She whipped out a jump rope with red handles and got to her feet. "Come on, Zoe. You take this end and I'll hold on to the other. Your daddy's going to jump first. You'll have to make big circles like I'm doing or the rope will hit him in the head."

"Oh, no—" Zoe cried.

"Don't worry," Dottie inserted. "Your daddy is a big boy. It won't hurt him."

So their visitor *had* noticed. Was that a negative in her eyes, too?

Zoe scrutinized him. "You're a boy?"

"Yes. He's a very big one," Dottie answered for him and his daughter laughed. Soon Zoe was using all her powers of concentration to turn the rope correctly and was doing an amazing job of it. After four times to get it right he heard, "You can jump in anytime now, Daddy."

Alex crouched down and managed to do two jumps

before getting caught around the shoulders. He was actually disappointed when their leader said, "Okay, now it's Zoe's turn. How many can you do?"

She cocked her dark brown head. "Five—"

"Well, that's something I want to see. Watch while we turn the rope. Whenever you think you're ready, jump in. It's okay if it takes you a whole bunch of times to do it, Zoe. Your daddy isn't going anywhere, right?"

She didn't look at him as she said it. He had a feeling it was on purpose.

"We're both in your hands for as long as it takes, Dorothy." He'd read the background information on her and knew it was her legal name.

"I never go by my given name," she said to Zoe without missing a beat while she continued to rotate the rope. "You can call me Dottie."

"That means crazy, doesn't it?" he threw out, curious to see how she'd respond.

"Your English vocabulary is remarkable, Your Highness."

"Is she crazy?" Zoe asked while she stood there, hesitant to try jumping.

"Be careful how you answer that," Dottie warned him. "Little royal pitchers have big ears and hers seem to be working just fine."

Alex couldn't help chuckling. He smiled at his daughter. "She's funny-crazy. Don't you think?"

"Yes." Zoe giggled again.

"Come on and jump." After eight attempts accompanied by a few tears, she finally managed a perfect jump. Dottie clapped her hands. "Good job, Zoe. Next time you'll do more."

She put the rope aside and reached into her bag of

tricks. His daughter wasn't the only one interested to see what she would pull out next. "For this game we have to get on our tummies."

The speech therapist might as well have been a magician. At this point his daughter was entranced and did what was suggested without waiting for Alex. In another minute Dottie had laid twenty-four cards facedown on the floor in four rows. She turned one card over. "Do you know what this is, Zoe?"

His daughter nodded. "Pig."

"Yes, and there's another card just like it. You have to remember where this card is, and then find the other one. When you do, then you make a book of them and put the pile to the side. You get one turn. Go ahead."

Zoe turned over another card.

"What is it?"

"Whale."

"Yes, but it's not a pig. So you have to put the card back. Okay, Daddy. It's your turn."

Alex turned over a card in the corner.

"Tiger, Daddy."

Before he could say anything, he saw their eyes look to the doorway. Alex turned around in frustration to see who had interrupted them.

"Hector?"

"Forgive me, Your Highness. There's a call for you from Argentum on an urgent matter that needs your attention."

Much as Alex hated to admit it, this had to be an emergency, otherwise Bari would have sent him an email. Barisou Jouflas was the head mining engineer on the island of Argentum and Alex's closest friend since college. He always enjoyed talking to him and got to his feet, expecting an outburst from Zoe. To his astonishment, Dottie had her completely engrossed in the matching game.

"I'll be back as soon as I can."

Dottie nodded without looking at him.

"Bye, Daddy," his daughter said, too busy looking for a matching card to turn her head.

Bye, Daddy— Since when? No tantrum because he was leaving?

Out of the corner of her eye Dottie watched the prince disappear and felt a twinge of disappointment for his daughter. They'd all been having fun and it was one time when he hadn't wanted to leave, she felt sure of it. But there were times when the affairs of the kingdom did have to take priority. Dottie understood that and forgave him.

He might be gone some time. Dottie still had other tests to do that she preferred to take place outside the palace. Now would be a good time to carry them out while Zoe was still amenable. Her speech was close to unintelligible, but she was bright as a button and Dottie understood most of what she was trying to say because of her years of training and personal experience.

Once they'd concluded the matching game she said, "Zoe? Do you want to come down to the beach with me?" The little girl clapped her hands in excitement.

"All right, then. Let's do it." Dottie got up and pulled a bag of items out of the bigger bag. "Shall we go down from here?"

"Yes!" Zoe stood up and started down the stairs at the far end of the patio. Dottie followed. The long stairway covering two stories led to the dazzling blue water below.

It was a warm, beautiful day. When they reached the beach, she pulled out a tube of sunscreen and covered both of them. Next she drew floppy sun hats from the bag for them to put on.

"Here's a shovel. Will you show me how you build a castle?"

Zoe got to work and made a large mound.

"That's wonderful. Now where do you think this flag should go?" She handed her a little one.

"Here!" She placed it on the very top.

"Perfect. Make a hole where the front door of the castle is located."

She made a big dent with her finger at the bottom. Dottie rummaged in the bag for a tiny sailboat and gave it to her. "This is your daddy's boat. Where do you think it goes?"

"Here." Zoe placed it at the bottom around the side.

"Good." Again Dottie reached in the bag and pulled out a plastic figure about one inch high. "Let's pretend this is your daddy. Where does he live in the castle?"

Zoe thought about it for a minute, then stuck him in the upper portion of the mound.

"And where do you sleep?" Dottie gave her a little female figure.

"Here." Zoe crawled around and pushed the figure into the mound at approximately the same level as the other.

"Do you sleep by your *Yiayia*?"

"No."

"Can you show me where she sleeps?" Dottie handed her another figure. Zoe moved around a little more and put it in at the same height. Everyone slept on the second floor.

"I like your castle. Let's take off our shoes and walk over to the water. Maybe we can find some pretty stones to decorate the walls. Here's a bucket to carry everything."

They spent the next ten minutes picking up tiny, multicolored stones. When they returned to the mound Dottie said, "Can you pour them on the sand and pick out the different colors? We'll put them in piles."

Zoe nodded, eager to sort everything. She was meticulous.

"Okay. Why don't you start with the pink stones and put them around the middle of the castle." Her little charge got the point in a hurry and did a masterful job. "Now place the orange stones near the top and the brown stones at the bottom."

While Zoe was finishing her masterpiece, Dottie took several pictures at different angles with her phone. "You'll have to show these pictures to your daddy. Now I think it's time to put our shoes on and go back to the palace. I'm hungry and thirsty and I bet you are, too. Here—let me brush the sand off your little piggies."

Zoe looked at her. "What?"

"These." She tugged on Zoe's toes. "These are your little pigs. Piggies. They go *wee wee wee*." She made a squealing sound.

When recognition dawned, laughter poured out of Zoe like tinkling bells. For just a moment it sounded like her little boy's laughter. Emotion caught Dottie by the throat.

"Mrs. Richards?" a male voice spoke out of the blue, startling her.

She jumped to her feet, fighting the tears pricking her eyelids, and looked around. A patrol boat had pulled up on the shore and she hadn't even heard it. Two men had converged on them, obviously guards protecting the palace grounds. "Yes?" She put her arm around Zoe's shoulders. "Is something wrong?"

"Prince Alexius has been looking for you. Stay here. He'll be joining you in a moment."

She'd done something wrong. Again.

No sooner had he said the words than she glimpsed the prince racing down the steps to the beach with the speed of a black panther in pursuit of its prey. The image sent a chill up her spine that raised the hairs on the back of her neck.

When he caught up to them, he gave a grim nod of dismissal to the guards, who got back in the patrol boat and took off.

"Look what I made, Daddy—" His daughter was totally unaware of the byplay.

Dottie could hear his labored breathing and knew it came from fright, not because he was out of shape. Anything but. While Zoe gave him a running commentary of their beach adventure in her inimitable way, Dottie put the bucket and shovel in the bag. When she turned around, she discovered him hunkered down, examining his daughter's work of art.

After listening to her intently, he lifted his dark head and shot Dottie a piercing black glance. Sotto voce, he said, "There are pirates in these waters who wait for an opportunity like this to—"

"I understand," she cut him off, feeling sick to her stomach. She'd figured it out before he'd said anything. "Forgive me. I swear it won't happen again."

"You're right about that."

His words froze the air in her lungs before he gripped his daughter's hand and started for the stairs.

"Come on," Zoe called to her.

Dottie followed, keeping her eyes on his hard-muscled physique clothed in a white polo shirt and dark blue trousers. Halfway up the stairs on those long, powerful legs, he gathered Zoe in his arms and carried her the rest of the way to the patio.

"The queen is waiting for Zoe to have lunch with her," he said when she caught up to him. "A maid is waiting outside my suite to conduct you back to your room. I've asked for a tray to be sent to you. We'll talk later."

Dottie heard Zoe's protests as he walked away. She gathered up the other bag and met the maid who accompanied her back to her own quarters. Once alone, she fled into the en suite bathroom and took a shower to wash off the sand and try to get her emotions under control.

No matter how unwittingly, she'd endangered the life of the princess. What if his little daughter had been kidnapped? It would have been Dottie's fault. All of it. The thought was so horrific, she couldn't bear it. The prince had every right to tell her she was leaving on the next flight to Athens.

This was one problem she didn't know how to fix. Being sorry wasn't enough. She'd wanted to make a difference in Zoe's life. The princess had passed every test with flying colors. Dottie was the one who'd never made the grade.

After drying off, she put on a white linen dress and sandals, prepared to be driven to the airport once the prince had told her he no longer required her services.

As she walked back into the bedroom, there was a knock on the door.

Dottie opened it to a maid who brought her a lunch tray and set it on the table in the alcove. She had no appetite but quenched her thirst with the flask of iced tea provided while she answered some emails from home. As she drained her second glass, there was another knock on the door.

"Hector?" she said after opening it. Somehow she wasn't surprised. He'd met her at the airport in Athens for her helicopter ride, and would deposit her at Hellenica's airport.

"Mrs. Richards. If you've finished your lunch, His Highness has asked me to take you to his office."

She deserved this. "I'm ready now."

By the time they reached it, she'd decided to leave today and would make it easy for the prince. But the room was empty. "Please be seated. His Highness will be with you shortly."

"Thank you." After he left, she sat on the love seat and waited. When the prince walked in, she jumped right back up again. "I'm so sorry for what happened today."

He seemed to have calmed down. "It's my fault for not having warned you earlier. There was a kidnapping attempt on Zoe at her preschool last fall."

"Oh, no—" Dottie cried out, aghast.

"Fortunately it failed. Since then I've tripled the security. It never occurred to me you would take Zoe down that long flight of stairs, even if it is our private beach. We can be grateful the patrol boats were watching you the entire time. You're as much a target as Zoe and you're my responsibility while you're here in Hellenica."

"I understand."

"Please be seated, Mrs. Richards."

"I—I can't," she stammered. Dottie bemoaned the fact that earlier during the testing, he'd called her Dorothy and had shown a teasing side to his nature. It had been unexpected and welcome. Right now those human moments out on the patio might never have been.

He eyed her up and down. "Have you injured yourself in some way?"

"You know I haven't," she murmured. "I wanted to tell you that you don't need to dismiss me because I'm leaving as soon as someone can drive me to the airport."

His black brows knit together in a fierce frown. "Whatever gave you the idea that your services are no longer required?"

She blinked in confusion. "*You* did, on the beach."

"Explain that to me," he demanded.

"When I swore to you that nothing like this would ever happen again, you said I was right about that."

His inky-black eyes had a laserlike quality. "So you jumped to the conclusion that I no longer trusted you with my daughter? Are you always this insecure?"

Dottie swallowed hard. "Only around monarchs who have to worry about pirates and kidnappers. I didn't know about those incidents and can't imagine how terrifying it must have been for you. When you couldn't find us today, it had to have been like déjà vu. I can't bear to think I caused you even a second's worry."

He took a deep breath. "From now on, whether with Zoe or alone, don't do anything without informing me of your intentions first. Then there won't be a problem."

"I agree." He was being much more decent about this than she had any right to expect. A feeling of admiration for his willingness to give her a second chance welled up inside her. When their eyes met again, she felt something almost tangible pass between them she couldn't explain, but it sent a sudden rush of warmth through her body, and she found herself unable to look away.

CHAPTER THREE

THE prince cleared his throat, breaking the spell. "After spending the day with my daughter, tell me what you've learned about her."

Dottie pulled herself together. The fear that she'd alienated the prince beyond salvaging almost made her forget why she'd come to Hellenica in the first place.

"I'll give you the bad news first. She has trouble articulating. Research tells us there are several reasons for it, but none of it matters. The fact is, she struggles with this problem.

"Now for the good news. Zoe is exceptionally intelligent with above-average motor and cognitive skills. Her vocabulary is remarkable. She understands prepositions and uses the right process to solve problems, such as in matching. Playing with her demonstrates her amazing dexterity. You saw her handling the balls and jumping rope. She has excellent coordination and balance.

"She follows directions the first time without problem. If you took a good look at that castle, it proves she sees things spatially. Her little mound had a first floor and a second floor, just like the palace. She understands her physical world and understands what she hears. Zoe only has one problem, as I said, but it's a big one since for the most part she can't make herself understood to anyone but you and the queen and, I presume to some extent, Sofia."

Alex nodded. "So that's why she's withdrawing from other people."

"Yes. You've told me she's been more difficult over the past few months. She's getting older and is losing her confidence around those who don't have her problem. She's smart enough to know she's different and not like everyone else. She wants to avoid situations that illuminate the difference, so she runs away and hides. It's the most natural instinct in the world.

"Zoe wants to make herself understood. The more she can't do it, the angrier she becomes, thus the tantrums. There's nothing wrong with her psychologically that wouldn't clear up immediately once she's free to express herself like everyone else does. She pushes people away and clings to you because you love her without qualification. But she knows the rest of the world doesn't love her, and she's feeling like a misfit."

The prince's sober expression masked a deep fear. She saw it in his eyes. "Can she overcome this?"

"Of course. She needs help saying all her sounds, but particularly the consonants. *H*'s and *T*'s are impossible for her. Few of her words come out right. Her frustration level has to be off the charts. But with constant work, she'll talk as well as I do."

He rubbed the back of his neck absently. "Are you saying you used to have the same problem?"

"I had a worse one. I stuttered so severely, I was the laughingstock of my classes in elementary school.

Children are cruel to other children. I used to pretend to be sick so I wouldn't have to go to school."

"How did you get through it?" He sounded pained for her.

"My aunt raised me. She was a stickler for discipline and sent me to a speech therapist every weekday, who taught me how to breathe, how to pace myself when I talked. After a few years I stuttered less and less. By high school it only showed up once in a while.

"Zoe has a different problem and needs to work on her sounds every day. If you could be the one encouraging her like a coach, she would articulate correct sounds faster. The more creativity, the better. I've brought toys and games you can play with her. While she's interacting with you, she'll learn to model her speech after you. Slowly but surely it will come."

"But you'll be here, too."

"Of course. You and I will work with her one on one, and sometimes the three of us will play together. I can't emphasize enough how much progress she'll make if you're available on a regular basis."

He shifted his weight. "How long do you think this will take?"

"Months to possibly several years. It's a gradual process and requires patience on everyone's part. When you feel confident, then another therapist can come in my place and—"

"I hired *you*," he interrupted her, underlining as never before that she was speaking to a prince.

"Yes, for the initial phase, but I'm a diagnostician and am needed other places."

His eyes narrowed on her face. "Is there a man in New York waiting for you to get back to him?"

No. That was a long time ago, she thought sorrowfully. Since then she'd devoted her time to her career. "Why does my personal life have to enter into this discussion?"

"I thought the point was obvious. You're young and attractive."

"Thank you. For that matter so are you, Your Highness, but you have more serious matters on your mind. So do I."

There she went again, speaking her thoughts out loud, offending him right and left. He studied her for a long time. "If it's money…"

"It's not. The Institute pays me well."

"Then?" He left the word hanging in the air.

"There is no *then*. You have your country to rule over. I have a career. The people with speech problems are *my* country. But for the time I'm here, I'll do everything in my power to get this program going for Zoe."

An odd tension had sprung between them. "Zoe only agreed to stop crying and eat lunch with the queen as long as she could return to the patio to play with you this afternoon," he said. "She had a better time with you this morning than I think she's ever had with anyone else."

Dottie smiled. "You mean besides you. That's because she was given the nonstop attention every child craves without being negatively judged. Would it be all right with you if she comes to my room for her lessons?"

"After the grilling you gave me, will I be welcome, too?" he countered in a silky voice that sent darts of awareness through her body. The prince was asking *her* permission after the outspoken way she'd just addressed him?

"I doubt Zoe will stay if you don't join us. Hopefully in a few days she'll come to my room, even when you can't be there. The alcove with the table makes it especially convenient for the games I've brought. If you'll make out a schedule and rules for me to follow, then there won't have to be so many misunderstandings on my part."

"Anything else?" She had a feeling he was teasing her now. This side of him revealed his charm and added to the depth of the man.

"Where does her Greek tutor teach her?"

"In the library, but she's developed an aversion to it and stays in her bedroom."

"That's what I used to do. It's where you can sleep and have no worries. In that room you can pretend you're normal like everyone else." Maybe it was a trick of light, but she thought she saw a glimmer of compassion radiate from those black depths. "As for your patio, I think it ought to remain your special treat for her."

"So do I. Why don't you go on up to your room. I'll bring Zoe in a few minutes. Later this evening you'll join me in the guest dining room near your suite and we'll discuss how you want to spend your time while you're in Hellenica when you're not with my daughter."

"That's very kind of you," Dottie murmured, but she didn't move because she didn't know if she'd been dismissed or not. When he didn't speak, she said, "Do I need to wait for a maid to escort me back to my room?"

His lips twitched, causing her breath to catch at the sight of such a beautiful man whose human side was doing things to her equilibrium without her consent. "Only if you're afraid you can't find it."

She stared into his eyes. "Thank you for trusting me. With work, Zoe's speech *will* improve."

On that note she left his office, feeling his all-seeing gaze on her retreating back. She hurried along the corridor on trembling legs and found the staircase back to the guest suite. Now that she'd discovered she was still employed by him, she was ravenous and ate the lunch she'd left on the tray.

Before he came with Zoe, she set things up to resemble a mini schoolroom; crayons, scissors, paper, building blocks, beads to string, hide-and-seek games, puzzles, sorting games. Flash cards. She'd brought several sets so he could keep a pack on him. All of it served as a device while she helped his daughter with her sounds.

That's why you're here, Dottie. It's the only reason. Don't ever forget it.

Alex found Dottie already seated in the guest dining room when he joined her that evening. She looked summery in a soft blue crochet top and white skirt that followed the lines and curves of her alluring figure.

He smiled. "May I join you?"

"Of course."

"You're sure?"

"I came from New York to try to be of help."

It wasn't the answer he'd wanted. In truth, he wasn't exactly sure what he wanted, but he felt her reserve around him when she wasn't with Zoe and was determined to get to the bottom of it. He sat down opposite her and within a minute their dinner was served.

Once they were alone again he said, "Whenever you wish to leave the palace, a car and driver will be at your disposal. Hector will arrange it. A bodyguard will always be with you. Hopefully you won't find my security people obtrusive."

"I'm sure I won't. Thank you." She began eating, but the silence stretched between them. Finally she said, "Could I ask you something without you thinking I'm criticizing you or stepping over the line?"

"Because I'm a prince?"

"Because you're a prince, a man and a father." She lifted her fabulous blue eyes to him. "I don't know which of those three people will be irked and maybe even angered."

Alex tried to keep a straight face. "I guess we won't know until I hear your question."

A sigh came out of her. "When did you stop eating dinner with Zoe as part of your natural routine?"

He hadn't seen that question coming. "After my wife died, I had to make up for a lot of missed work in my capacity as overseer of the mining industry of our country. Hellenica couldn't have the high quality of life it enjoys without the revenue paid by other countries needing our resources. It requires constant work and surveillance.

"I spent my weekends with Zoe, but weekdays my hours were long, so she ate dinner with her nannies and my grandmother, who could get around then and spent a lot of her time on Aurum with us. However, I never missed kissing my daughter good-night and putting her to bed. That routine has gradually become the norm.

"With Stasio gone the past six weeks, I've had to be here and have been stretched to the max with monarchy business plus my own work."

"Do you mind if I ask what it is you do for your

brother? I've often wondered what a crown prince's daily routine is really like."

"Let me put it this way. On top of working with the ministers while he runs the complex affairs of our country on a daily basis, Stasio has at least four hundred events to attend or oversee during a year's time. That's more than one a day where he either gives a speech, entertains international dignitaries, attends openings or christens institutions, all while promoting the general welfare of Hellenica."

"It's very clear his life isn't his own. Neither is yours, obviously. Where did you go today after our session with Zoe?"

Alex was surprised and pleased she'd given him that much thought. "I had to fly to one of the islands in the north to witness the installation of the new president of the Thracian college and say a few words in Stasio's place. I should have stayed for the dinner, but I told them I had another engagement I couldn't miss." Alex had wanted to eat dinner with her. He enjoyed her company.

"Do you like your work? I know that probably sounds like an absurd question, but I'm curious."

"Like all work, it has its good and bad moments, but if I were honest I'd have to say that for the most part I enjoy it—very much, in fact, when something good happens that benefits the citizenry. After a lot of work and negotiations, four new hospitals will be under construction shortly. One of them will be a children's hospital. Nothing could please me more."

"Does Zoe know about this hospital? Do you share some of the wonderful things you do when you're with her?"

Her question surprised him. "Probably not as much as I should," he answered honestly.

"The reason I asked is because if she understood what kinds of things take up your time when you're away from her, she'd be so proud of you and might not feel as much separation anxiety when you're apart."

He looked at her through shuttered eyes. "If I didn't know better, I'd think you were a psychiatrist."

She let out a gentle laugh. "Hardly. You appear to have an incredible capacity to carry your brother's load as well as your own and still see to your daughter's needs. I'm so impressed."

"But?"

"I didn't say anything."

"You didn't have to. It's there in your expression. If I ate dinner with my daughter every evening, her speech would come faster."

"Maybe a little, but I can see you're already burning the candle at both ends out of concern for your country and necessity. It would be asking too much of you when you're already making time for her teaching sessions." She sat back. "I'm so sorry you lost your wife, who must have been such a help to you. It must have been a terrible time for you."

"It was, but I had Zoe. Her smiling face made me want to get up in the morning when I didn't think I could."

Moisture filmed her eyes. "I admire you for the wonderful life you're giving her."

"She's worth everything to me. You do what you have to do. Don't forget I've had a lot of help from family and the staff."

"Even so, your little Zoe adores you. It means whatever you're doing is working." She pushed herself away from the table and got to her feet. "Good night, Your Highness. No, no. Don't get up. Enjoy that second cup of coffee in peace.

"What with worrying about your grandmother, too, you deserve a little pampering. From my vantage point, no one seems to be taking care of you. In all the fairy tales I read as a child, they went to the castle and lived happily ever after. Until now I never thought about the prince's welfare."

Her comment stunned him before she walked out of the dining room.

Two nights later, while Alex was going over a new schedule he'd been working out with his internal affairs minister, a maid came into his office with a message. He wasn't surprised when he heard what was wrong. In fact he'd half been expecting it.

"If you'll excuse me."

"Of course, Your Highness."

Pleased that he'd been able to arrange his affairs so he could eat dinner with Zoe and Dottie from now on, he got up from the desk and headed for Zoe's bedroom. He heard crying before he opened the door. Poor Sofia was trying to calm his blotchy-faced daughter, who took one look at him and flung herself against his body.

Alex gathered her in his arms. "What's the matter?" he asked, knowing full well what was wrong. She'd been having the time of her life since Dottie had come to the palace and she didn't want the fun to stop.

Sofia shook her head. "She was asleep, and then suddenly she woke up with a nightmare. I haven't been able to quiet her down, Your Highness. She doesn't want me to help her anymore."

"I understand. It's all right. You can retire now. Thank you."

After she went into the next room, where she'd been sleeping lately, Zoe cried, "I want my mommy."

She'd never asked for her mother before. From time to time they'd talked about Teresa. He'd put pictures around so she would always know what her mother looked like, but this was different. He pulled one of them off the dresser and put it in her hand. To his shock, she pushed the photo away. "I want Dot. She's my mommy."

Alex was aghast. His daughter had shortened Dottie's name, but the sound that came out would make no sense to anyone except Alex, who understood it perfectly. "No, Zoe. Dottie's your teacher."

She had that hysterical look in her eyes. "No—she's my mommy. Where did she go?"

"Your mommy's in heaven."

"No—" She flung her arms around his neck. "Get my mommy!"

"I can't, Zoe."

"Has she gone?" The fright in her voice stunned him.

Alex grabbed the photograph. "This is your mommy. She went to heaven, remember?"

"Is Dot in heaven?"

Obviously his daughter's dreaming had caused her to awaken confused. "Dottie is your teacher and she went to her room, but she's not your mommy."

"Yes, she is." She nodded. "She's my new mommy!" she insisted before breaking down in sobs.

New?

"I want her! Get her, Daddy! Get her!" she begged him hysterically.

Feeling his panic growing, he pulled out his cell phone to call Hector.

"Your Highness?"

"Finds Mrs. Richards and tell her to come to Zoe's suite immediately."

"I'll take care of it now."

Alex could be thankful there was no one more efficient than Hector in an emergency.

When Dottie walked into the room a few minutes later with a book in her hand, his daughter had calmed down somewhat, but was still shuddering in his arms.

"Dot—" Zoe blurted with such joy, Alex was speechless.

"Hi, Zoe. Did you want to say good-night?"

"Yes."

"She thought you were gone," Alex whispered in an aside.

Dottie nodded. "Why don't you get in bed and I'll read you a story. Then *I* have to go to bed, too, because you and I have a big day planned for tomorrow, don't we?"

Zoe's lips turned up in a smile. "Yes."

Like magic, his daughter crawled under the covers. Dottie pulled up a chair next to the bed. "This is the good-night book. See the moon on the cover? When he's up there, everyone goes to sleep. Freddie the frog stops going *ribbbbbit* and says good-night." Zoe laughed.

Dottie turned the page. "Benny the bee stops *buzzzz-ing* and says good-night." She showed each page to his daughter who was enchanted. "Charlie the cricket stops *chirrrping* and says good-night. Guess who's on the last page?" Zoe didn't know. Dottie showed it to her. There was a mirror. "It's *you!* Now *you* have to say good-night."

Zoe said it.

"Let's say the *g* again. Mr. G is a grumpy letter." Zoe thought that was hilarious. "He gets mad." She made a face. "Let's see if we can get as mad as he does. We have to grit our teeth like this. Watch my mouth and say *grrr.*"

Alex was watching it. To his chagrin he'd been watching it on and off for several days. After half a dozen tries Zoe actually made the *grrr* sound. He couldn't believe it. In his astonishment his gaze darted to Dottie, but she was focused on his daughter.

"You sounded exactly like Mr. G, Zoe. That was perfect. Tomorrow night your father will read it to you again. Now Dot has to go to sleep. I'll leave the book with you." She slipped out of the room, leaving the two of them alone.

Zoe clasped it to her chest as if it were her greatest treasure. Alex's eyes smarted because lying before him was *his* greatest treasure. She fell asleep within minutes. As soon as she was out, he left the room knowing Sofia was sleeping in the adjacent room and would hear her if she woke up.

He strode through the palace, intending to talk to Dottie before she went to bed. Hector met him as he was passing his grandmother's suite on his way to the other wing.

"The queen wants to see you before she retires."

His brows lifted. "You wouldn't by any chance be spying on me for her, would you, Hector?"

"I have never spied on you, Your Highness."

"You've been spying for her since the day Stasi and I were born, but I forgive you. However, Stasi might not be so forgiving once he's crowned, so remember you've been warned. Tell the queen I'll be with her in ten minutes."

He continued on his way to Dottie's apartment. After he knocked, she called out, "Yes?"

"It's Alex."

The silence that followed was understandable. He'd never used his given name with her before, or given his permission for her to use it. But considering the amount of time they'd been spending together since her arrival at the palace, it seemed absurd to say anything else now that they were alone. "Would you be more willing to answer me if I'd said it's Zoe's father, or it's your Royal Highness?"

He thought he heard her chuckle before she opened the door a couple of inches. "I was on the verge of crawling into bed."

Alex could see that. She'd thrown on a pink toweling robe and was clutching the lapels beneath her chin. "I need to talk frankly with you. Zoe has decided you're her new mommy. She got hysterical tonight when I tried to tell her otherwise."

"I know. She's told me on several occasions she wishes I were her mother. This happens with some of my youngest students who don't have one. It's very normal. I just keep telling them I'm their teacher. You need to go on telling her in a matter-of-fact way that Princess Teresa was her mommy."

"I did that."

"I know. I saw the photograph and see a lot of the princess's beauty in Zoe. What's important here is that if you don't fight her on it, she'll finally get the point and the phase will pass after a while."

"That's very wise counsel." He exhaled the breath he'd been holding. "You made a breakthrough with her tonight."

"Yes. I've wanted her to feel confident about one sound and now it has happened."

"How did you know she would do it?"

"I didn't, but I hoped. Every success creates more success."

Talking through the crack in the door added a certain intimacy to their conversation, exciting him. "Her success is going to help me sleep tonight."

"I'm glad. Just remember a total change isn't going to happen overnight. Her vowels are coming, but *G* is only one consonant out of twenty-one. Putting that sound with the rest of a word is the tricky part."

"Tricky or not, she mimicked you perfectly and the way you read that book had her spellbound."

"There was only one thing wrong with it."

"What's that?" He found himself hanging on her every word, just like his daughter.

"It didn't have a page that said the prince stopped *rrrrruling* and said good-night."

Alex broke into full-bodied laughter.

Her eyes smiled. "If you'll forgive me, you should do that more often in front of Zoe, Your Highness."

"What happened to Alex? That is my name."

"I realize that."

"Before I leave, I wanted you to know that I've worked things out with my internal affairs minister so I can eat dinner with my daughter every night. From now on he'll take care of the less important matters for me during that time period."

"Zoe's going to be ecstatic!" she blurted, displaying the bubbly side of her nature that didn't emerge as often as he would have liked to see.

"I hope that means you're happy about it, too, since you'll be joining us for our meals. Good night, Dottie."

"Good night, Alex."

She shut the door on him before he was ready to leave. After being with her, he wasn't in the mood to face his grandmother. As he made his way back to her suite, he thought about his choice of words. The only time he'd ever *faced* the queen was when he'd been a boy and had a reason to feel guilty about something.

Tonight he had a strong hunch what she wanted to discuss with him. After Zoe's nightmare, now he knew why. If she'd told *Yiayia* that Dottie was her new mommy, nothing would have enraged his grandmother more. She would have told Zoe never to speak of it again, but that wouldn't prevent his daughter from thinking it in her heart.

Until the phase passed, Dottie had said.

What if it didn't? That's what disturbed Alex.

Zoe's insistence that Dottie was her new mommy only exacerbated his inner conflict where the speech therapist was concerned. Since he'd peered into a pair of eyes as blue as the flowers fluttering in the breeze around the palace in Aurum, he couldn't get her out of his mind.

In truth he had no business getting physically involved with someone he'd hired. He certainly didn't need the queen reminding him of what he'd already been telling himself—keep the relationship with Mrs.

Richards professional and enjoy the other women he met when he left the country for business or pleasure.

Too bad for his grandmother that he saw through her machinations and had done so from an early age. She always had another agenda going. Since Teresa's funeral, she'd been busy preparing the ground with the House of Helvetia. But until Stasi married, she was biding her time before she insisted Alex take Princess Genevieve of Helvetia to wife for the growth and prosperity of the kingdom.

Lines darkened his face. The queen would have to bide away forever because Stasi would be the only one doing the growing for the Constantinides dynasty. He was the firstborn, Heaven had picked him to rule Hellenica. Ring out the bells.

Alex had a different destiny and a new priority that superseded all else. He wanted to help his daughter feel normal, and that meant coaching her. With Dottie's help, it was already happening. She understood what was going on inside Zoe. Her story about her own stuttering problem had touched him. He admired her strength in overcoming a huge challenge.

His first order of business was to talk to Stasio tonight. His brother needed to come home now! With Alex's work schedule altered, he could spend the maximum amount of time with Zoe and Dottie throughout the day. It was going to work, even though it meant dealing with his ministers in the early morning hours and late at night when necessary.

Once Stasio was home, Alex would move back to the island of Aurum, where he could divide his attention between helping Zoe and doing the work he'd been overseeing for the country since university. With Dottie installed and a palace staff and security waiting on them, Zoe couldn't help but make great strides with her speech and he'd convince Dottie she couldn't leave yet.

CHAPTER FOUR

LIKE pizza dough being tossed in the air, Dottie's heart did its own version of a flip when the prince entered her schoolroom a few days later with Zoe. They must have just come from breakfast with the queen. Zoe was dressed in pink play clothes and sneakers.

Dottie hardly recognized Alex. Rather than hand-tooled leather shoes, he'd worn sneakers, too. She was dazzled by his casual attire of jeans and a yellow, open-necked sport shirt. In the vernacular, he was a hunk. When she looked up and saw the smattering of dark hair on his well-defined chest, her mouth went dry and she averted her eyes. Zoe's daddy was much more man than prince this morning, bringing out longings in her she hadn't experienced in years.

He'd been coming to their teaching sessions and had cleared his calendar to eat dinner with Zoe. Dottie was moved by his love and concern for his daughter, but she feared for him, too. The prince had the greatest expectations for his child, but he might want too much too soon. That worry had kept her tossing and turning during the night because she wanted to be up to the challenge and help Zoe triumph.

But it wasn't just that worry. When she'd told Alex

she'd had other patients who'd called her mommy, it was a lie. Only one other child had expressed the same wish. It was a little boy who had a difficult, unhappy mother. In truth, Zoe was unique. So was the whole situation.

Normally Dottie's students came by bus or private car to the institute throughout the day. Living under the palace roof was an entirely different proposition and invited more intimacy. Zoe was a very intelligent child and should have corrected her own behavior by now, but she chose to keep calling Dottie Mommy. Every time Zoe did that, it blurred the lines for Dottie, who in a short time had allowed the little girl to creep into her heart.

To make matters worse, Dottie was also plagued by guilt because she realized she wanted Alex's approval. That sort of desire bordered on pride. Her aunt had often quoted Gibran. "Generosity is giving more than you can, and pride is taking less than you need." If she wanted his approval, then it was a gift she had to earn.

Did she seek it because he was a prince? She hoped not. Otherwise that put her in the category of those people swayed by a person's station in life. She refused to be a sycophant, the kind of person her aunt had despised. Dottie despised sycophants, too.

"GGGRRRRRR," she said to Zoe, surprising the little girl, who was a quick study and *gggrrrred* back perfectly. Alex gave his daughter a hug before they sat down at the table.

"Wonderful, Zoe." Her gaze flicked to him. "Good morning, Your Highness." Dottie detected the scent of the soap he'd used in the shower. It was the most marvelous smell, reminding her of mornings when her husband—

But the eyes staring at her across the table were a fiery black, not blue. "Aren't you going to *gggrrr* me? I feel left out."

Her pulse raced. "Well, we don't want you to feel like that, do we, Zoe?" The little girl shook her head, causing her shiny brown curls to flounce.

Dottie had a small chalkboard and wrote the word *Bee.* "Go ahead and pronounce this word for us, Your Highness." When he did, she said, "Zoe? Did you hear *bee*?"

"Yes."

"Good. Let's all say *bee* together. One, two three. *Bee.*" Zoe couldn't do it, of course. Dottie leaned toward her. "Pretend you're a tiny goldfish looking for food." Pressing her lips together she made the beginning of the *B* sound. "Touch my lips with your index finger." Her daddy helped her. In the process his fingers brushed against Dottie's mouth. She could hardly breathe from the sensation of skin against skin.

"Now feel how it sounds when I say it." Dottie said it a dozen times against Zoe's finger. She giggled. "That tickled, didn't it? Now say the same sound against my finger." She put her finger to Zoe's lips. After five tries she was making the sound.

"Terrific! Now put your lips to your daddy's finger and make the same *B* sound over and over."

As Zoe complied with every ounce of energy in that cute little body, Alex caught Dottie's gaze. The softness, the gratitude she saw in his eyes caused her heart to hammer so hard, she feared he could hear it.

"You're an outstanding pupil, Zoe. Today we're going to work on the *B* sound."

"It's interesting you've brought up the *bee*," Alex interjected.

"They make honey," said Zoe.

"That's right, Zoe. Did you know that just yesterday I met with one of the ministers and we're going to establish beekeeping centers on every island in Hellenica."

"How come?"

"With more bees gathered in hives, we'll have more honey to sell to people here as well as around the world. It's an industry I'd like to see flourish. With all the blossoms and thyme that grow here, it will give jobs to people who don't have one. You know the honey you eat when we're on Aurum?" She nodded. "It comes from two hives Inez and Ari tend on our property."

Zoe's eyes widened. "They do? I've never seen them."

"When we go home, we'll take a look."

Zoe smiled and gave her father a long hug. As he reciprocated, his gaze met Dottie's. He'd taken her suggestion to share more with his daughter and it was paying dividends, thrilling her to pieces.

"I'm going to give your daddy a packet of flash cards, Zoe. Everything on it starts with a *B*. He'll hold up the card and say the word. Then you say it. If you can make three perfect *B* sounds, I have a present for you."

Zoe let out a joyous sound and looked at her daddy with those shiny brown eyes. Dottie sat back in the chair and watched father and daughter at work. Zoe had great incentive to do her best for the man she idolized. The prince took his part seriously and proceeded with care. She marveled to watch them drawing closer together through these teaching moments, forging closer bonds now that he was starting to ease up on his work for the monarchy.

"Bravo!" she said when he'd gone through the pack of thirty. "You said five *B*'s clearly. Do you want your present now or after your lesson?"

Zoe concentrated for a minute. "Now."

Alex laughed that deep male laugh. It resonated through Dottie to parts she'd forgotten were there. Reaching in the bag in the corner, she pulled out one of several gifts she'd brought for rewards. But this one was especially vital because Zoe had been working hard so far and needed a lot of reinforcement.

Dottie handed her the soft, foot-long baby. "This is Baby Betty. She has a *bottle*, a *blanket* and a *bear*."

"Oh—" Zoe cried. Her eyes lit up. She cradled it in her arms, just like a mother. "Thank you, Mommy."

The word slipped out again. Dottie couldn't look at Alex. His daughter had said it again. These days it was coming with more frequency. The moment had become an emotional one for Dottie, who had to fight her own pain over past memories that had been resurrected by being around her new student.

"I'm not your mommy, Zoe. She's in heaven. You know that, don't you."

She finally nodded. "I wish you were my mommy."

"But since I'm not, will you please call me Dot?"

"Yes."

"Good girl. Guess what? Now that you've fed Betty, you have to burp her." Puzzled, Zoe looked up at her. "When a baby drinks milk from a bottle, it drinks in air, too. So you have to pat her back. Then the air will come out and she won't have a tummyache. Your mommy used to pat your back like that when you were a baby, didn't she, Your Highness?"

Dottie had thrown the ball in his court, not knowing what had gone on in their marriage. He'd never discussed his private personal life or asked Dottie about hers.

"Indeed, she did. We took turns walking the floor with you. Sometimes very important people would come in the nursery to see you and you'd just yawn and go to sleep as if you were horribly bored."

At that comment the three of them laughed hard. Dottie realized it provided a release from the tension built up over the last week.

From the corner of her eye she happened to spot Hector, who stood several feet away. He was clearing his throat to get their attention. How long had he been in the room listening?

"Your Highness? The queen has sent for you."

"Is it a medical emergency?"

"No."

"Then I'm afraid she'll have to wait until tonight. After this lesson I'm taking Zoe and Mrs. Richards out on the *boat*," he said emphasizing the B. "We'll work on her *B* sounds while we enjoy a light *buffet* on *board*, won't we, Zoe?" He smiled at his daughter who nodded, still gripping her baby tightly. "But don't worry. I'll be back in time to say good-night to her."

"Very well, Your Highness."

Dottie had to swallow the gasp that almost escaped her throat. Lines bracketed Hector's mouth. She looked at the floor. It really was funny. Alex had a quick, brilliant mind and a surprising imp inside him that made it hard for her to hold back her laughter, but she didn't dare laugh in front of Hector.

After Hector left, Dottie brought out a box containing tubes of blue beads, so Zoe and Alex could make a bracelet together. They counted the beads as they did so, and Dottie was pleased to note that Zoe's *B* sounds were really coming along.

Satisfied with that much progress, Dottie cleaned everything up. "That's the end of our lesson for today." She got up from the chair, suddenly wishing she weren't wearing a T-shirt with a picture of a cartoon bunny on the front. She'd hoped Zoe would ask her about it and they could practice saying the famous rabbit's name. But it was Alex who'd stared at it several times this morning, causing sensual waves to ripple through her.

He swept Zoe in his arms. "I'm very proud of you. Now let's show Dot around the island on the sailboat." His daughter hugged him around the neck. Over her shoulder he stared at Dottie. "Are you ready?"

No. Sailing with him wasn't part of her job. In fact it was out of the question. She didn't want to feel these feelings she had around him. Yearnings...

"That's very kind of you, Your Highness, but I have other things to do this afternoon, including a lot of paperwork to send in to the Institute. In case you don't get back from sailing by dinnertime, I'll see you and Zoe in the morning for her lesson."

He lowered his daughter to the floor. "I insist."

She took a steadying breath. "Did you just give me a command?"

"If I did, would you obey it?"

There was nothing playful about this conversation. The last thing she wanted to do was offend him, but she refused to be anything but Zoe's speech therapist. With his looks and charismatic personality, he could ensnare any woman he wanted. That's what royal playboys did.

Alex might be a widower with a daughter, but as far as she was concerned, he was at the peak of his manhood now and a hundred times more dangerous. She was reminded of that fact when he'd eyed her T-shirt. A little shiver went through her because he was still eyeing her that way and she was too aware of him.

Dottie needed to turn this around and make it right so he wouldn't misunderstand why she was refusing the invitation. Using a different tactic she said, "I gave you that pack of flash cards. You should take your daughter on your sailboat this afternoon and work with her while the lesson is fresh in her mind."

In a lowered voice she added, "I might be her speech therapist, but outside this classroom I can only be a distraction and cause her more confusion over the mommy issue. She wants your undivided attention and will cooperate when you do the cards with her because she'd do anything for you. There's a saying in English. I'm sure you've heard of it. 'Strike while the iron's hot.'"

"There's another saying by the great teacher Plato," he fired back. "'We can easily forgive a child who is afraid of the dark; the real tragedy of life is when men are afraid of the light.'" He turned to his daughter. "Come with me, Zoe."

Dottie trembled as she watched them leave. Alex had her figured out without knowing anything about her. She *was* afraid. Once upon a time her world had been filled with blinding, glorious light. After it had been taken away, she never wanted to feel it or be in it again. One tragedy in life had been too much.

* * *

Alex put his daughter to bed, but he had to face facts. After the outing on the sailboat and all the swimming and fun coaching moments with the flash cards, it still wasn't enough for his little girl. She didn't want Sofia tending to her.

He'd read the good-night book to her six times, but the tears gushed anyway. She was waiting for her favorite person. "Have you forgotten that Dottie had a lot of work to do tonight? You'll see her in the morning. Here's Betty. She's ready to go to sleep with you." He tucked the baby in her arm, but she pushed it away and sat up.

"Tell Dot to come."

Alex groaned because these tears were different. His daughter had found an outlet for her frustration in Dottie who understood her and had become her ally. What child wouldn't want her to be her mommy and stay with her all the time? Alex got it. She made every moment so memorable, no one else could possibly measure up. Dottie was like a force of nature. Her vivacious personality had brought life into the palace.

Earlier, when he'd asked Hector about Dottie's activities, he'd learned she'd refused a car and had left the grounds on foot. Security said that after she'd jogged ten miles in the heat, she'd hiked to the top of Mount Pelos and sat for an hour. After visiting the church, she'd returned to town and jogged back to the palace.

"Zoe? If you'll stay in your bed, I'll go get her."

The tears slowed down. She reached for her baby. "Hurry, Daddy."

Outside the bedroom he called Dottie on his cell phone, something he'd sworn he wouldn't do in order to keep his distance, but this was an emergency. When she picked up, he asked her to come to Zoe's bedroom.

He sensed the hesitation before she said, "I'll be right there."

It pleased him when a minute later he heard footsteps and watched Dottie hurrying towards the suite with another book in her hand.

"Alex—" she cried in surprise as he stepped away from the paneled wall.

He liked it that she'd said his name of her own volition. "I wondered when you would finally break down."

Dottie smoothed the hair away from her flushed cheek. Her eyes searched his. Ignoring his comment she said, "Did Zoe have another nightmare?"

He moved closer. "No. But she's growing more and more upset when you're not with us. Why didn't you come today? I want the truth."

"I told you I had work."

"Then how come it was reported that you went jogging and climbed Mount Pelos, instead of staying in your room? Were you able to see the sail of my boat from the top?"

A hint of pink crept into her cheeks. She *had* been watching for him. "I saw a lot of sailboats."

"The security staff is agog about the way you spent your day. Not one visit to a designer shop. No shopping frenzy. You undoubtedly wore them to a frazzle with your jogging, but it was good for them."

A small laugh escaped her throat. He liked it that she didn't take herself seriously.

"I'll ask the question again. Why didn't you come with us this afternoon?"

"Surely you know why. Because I'm worried over her growing attachment to me."

"So am I, but that's not the only reason you kept your distance from me today. Are you afraid of being on a boat? Don't you know how to swim?"

"Don't be silly," she whispered.

"How else am I to get some honesty out of you? It's apparent you have a problem with me, pure and simple. My earlier reputation in life as Prince Alexius may have prejudiced you against me, but that was a long time ago. I'm a man now and a father the world knows nothing about. Which of those roles alarms you most?"

She folded her arms. "Neither of them," she said in a quiet voice.

His brows met in a frown. "Then what terrible thing do you imagine would have happened to you today if you'd come with us?"

"I'd rather not talk about it, even if you are a prince." She'd said that "even if you are a prince" thing before. After retaining his gaze for a moment, she looked away. "How did your afternoon go with Zoe?"

"Good, but it would have been better if you'd been along. She won't go to sleep until you say good-night. Tonight she fired Sofia."

"What?"

"It's true. She doesn't want a nanny unless it's you. To save poor Hector the trouble of having to summon you every night, why don't you plan to pop in on her at bedtime. In the end it will save my sanity, too."

She slowly nodded. "Since I won't be here much longer, I can do that."

"Let's not talk about your leaving, not when you barely got here."

"I—I'll go in now." Her voice faltered.

"Thank you." For several reasons, he wasn't through with her yet, but it could wait until she'd said good-night to his daughter. Alex followed her into the bedroom. Zoe was sitting up in her bed holding her baby. She glowed after she saw Dottie.

"Hi, Zoe. If I read you a story, will you go to sleep?"

"Yes. Will you sit on the bed?"

"I can read better on this chair." Dottie drew it close to the bed and sat down. Once again Alex was hooked by Dottie's charm as she read the tale about a butterfly that had lost a wing and needed to find it.

She was a master teacher, but it dawned on him she always kept her distance with Zoe. No hugs or kisses. No endearments. Being the total professional, she knew her place. Ironically his daughter didn't want hugs or kisses from her nannies who tried to mother her, but he knew she was waiting for both from Dottie.

Zoe wasn't the only one.

The second she'd gone to sleep, Dottie tiptoed out of the room. Alex caught up to her in the hall. She couldn't seem to get back to her suite fast enough. They walked through the corridors in silence. As she reached out to open the door to her apartment, he grasped her upper arms and turned her around.

They were close enough he could smell her peach fragrance. She was out of breath, but she was in too good a shape for the small exertion of walking to produce that reaction. "Invite me in," he whispered, sensing how withdrawn she'd become with him. "I want an answer from you and prefer that we don't talk out here in the hall where we can be observed."

"I'm sorry, but we have nothing to talk about. I'm very tired."

"Too tired to tell me what has you so frightened, you're trembling?"

A pained expression crossed over her face. "I wish I hadn't come to Hellenica. If I'd known what was awaiting me, I would have refused."

"For the love of heaven, why? If I've done something unforgivable in your eyes, it's only fair you tell me."

"Of course you haven't." She shook her head, but wouldn't look at him. "This has to do with Zoe."

"Because she keeps calling you Mommy?"

"That and much more."

At a total loss, he let go of her with reluctance. "I don't understand."

She eased away from him. "Five years ago my husband and son were killed by a drunk driver in a horrific crash." Tears glistened on her cheeks. "I lost the great loves of my life. Cory was Zoe's age when he died."

Alex was aghast.

"He had an articulation problem like hers, only he couldn't do his vowel sounds. I'd been working with him for a year with the help of a therapist, and he'd just gotten to the point where he could say *Daddy* plainly when—"

Obviously she was too choked up to say the rest. His eyes closed tightly for a moment. He remembered the pain in hers the other day.

"I've worked with all kinds of children, but Zoe is the only one who has ever reminded me of him. The other day when she laughed, it sounded like Cory."

"You didn't let on." His voice grated.

"I'm thankful for that." He thought he heard a little

sob get trapped in her throat. "It's getting harder to be around her without breaking down. That's why I didn't go with you today. I—I thought I'd gotten past my grief," she stammered, "but coming here has proven otherwise."

He sucked in his breath. "You may wish you hadn't come to Hellenica, but keep in mind you're doing something for my daughter only you can do. Watching Zoe respond to your techniques has already caused me to stop grieving over her pain.

"No matter how much you're still mourning your loss, doesn't it make you feel good to be helping her the way you once helped your son? Wouldn't your husband have done anything for your son if your positions were reversed?"

She looked away, moved by his logic. "Yes," came the faint whisper, "but—"

"But what? Tell me everything."

"It's just that I've felt…guilty for not being with them that terrible day."

"You're suffering survivor's guilt."

"Yes."

"In my own way I had the same reaction after Teresa passed away. It took me a long time to convince myself everything possible had been done for her and I had to move on for Zoe's sake."

She nodded.

"Then it's settled. From now on after her morning lessons, we'll have another one during the afternoons in the swimming pool. We'll practice what you've taught her while we play. After finding your strength and solace in furthering your career, don't you see you can make a difference with Zoe and maybe lay those ghosts to rest? It's time to take a risk. With my schedule changed, I can spend as much time as possible with both of you now."

"I've noticed." After a pause, she added, "You're a remarkable man."

"It's because of you, Dottie. You're helping me get close to my daughter in a whole new way. I'll never be able to thank you enough for that."

"You don't need to thank me. I'm just so glad for the two of you." Dottie wiped the moisture from the corners of her eyes. "Tomorrow we'll work on her *W* sounds. Good night, Alex."

CHAPTER FIVE

What luxury! Dottie had never known anything like it until she'd come to the palace ten days ago. After a delicious lunch, it was sheer bliss to lie in the sun on the lounger around the palace pool enjoying an icy fruit drink.

Zoe's morning lesson with her daddy had gone well. Her *B* and G sounds were coming along, but she struggled with the *W*. It might be one of the last sounds she mastered on her long journey to intelligible speech.

Dottie was glad to have the pool to herself. While they were changing into their swimsuits, she was trying to get a grip on her emotions. She'd been doing a lot of thinking, and Alex had been right about one thing. If she'd been the one killed and Cory had been left with his speech problem, then she would have wanted Neil to stop at nothing to find the right person to help their son. At the moment, Dottie was the right person for Zoe.

Deep in her own thoughts, she heard a tremendous splash followed by Zoe's shriek of laughter. Dottie turned her head in time to see Zoe running around the rim of the pool in her red bathing suit, shouting with glee. She was following a giant black whale maybe five feet long skimming the top of the water with a human torpedo propelling it.

Suddenly Alex's dark head emerged, splashing more water everywhere. Zoe got soaked and came flying toward Dottie, who grabbed her own towel and wiped off her shoulders. "You need some sunscreen. Stand still and I'll put it on you." Zoe did her bidding. "I didn't know a whale lived in your pool."

The child giggled. "Come with me." She tugged on Dottie's arm.

"I think I'd rather stay here and watch."

Alex stared at Dottie with a look she couldn't decipher, but didn't say anything. By now Zoe had joined him and was riding on top of the whale while he helped her hold on. The darling little girl was so happy, she seemed to burst with it.

Dottie threw her beach wrap around her to cover her emerald-colored bikini and got up from the lounger. She walked over to the side of the pool and sat down to dangle her legs in the water while she watched their antics.

All of a sudden it occurred to her she was having real fun for the first time in years. This was different than watching from the sidelines of other people's lives. Because of Alex she was an actual participant and was feeling a part of life again. The overpowering sense of oneness with him shook her to the core. So did the desire she felt being near him. That's why she didn't dare get in the water. Her need to touch him was overcoming her good sense.

"I think we need to name Zoe's whale," he called to her.

Dottie nodded. "Preferably a two syllable word starting with *W*."

Both she and Alex suggested a lot of names, laughing into each other's eyes at some of their absurd suggestions. Zoe clapped her hands the minute she heard her daddy say *Wally*. Though it wasn't a name that started with *Wh* like whale, it was the name his daughter wanted. When Zoe pronounced it, the sound came out like *Oye-ee*.

Dottie was secretly impressed when he came up with the idea of Zoe pretending she was a grouper fish. Evidently his daughter knew what one looked like and she formed her mouth in an *O* shape, opening and closing it. After a half hour of playing and practice, the *wa* was starting to make an appearance.

"Well done, Your Highness." Dottie smiled at him. "She wouldn't have made that sound this fast without your help."

He reciprocated with a slow, lazy smile, making jelly of her insides. The afternoon was exhilarating for Dottie, a divine moment out of time. Anyone watching would think they were a happy family. Before she knew it, dinner was served beneath the umbrella of the table on the sun deck. Zoe displayed a healthy appetite, pleasing her father and Dottie.

Toward the end of their meal he said, "Attention, everyone. I have an announcement to make." He looked at Zoe. "Guess who came home today?"

She stopped drinking her juice. "Uncle Stasi?"

"Yes. Your one and only favorite uncle."

"Goody!" she blurted. "He's funny."

"I've missed him, too. Tonight there's going to be a

party to welcome him back. I'm going to take you two ladies with me."

Zoe squealed in delight.

"After we finish dinner, I want you to go upstairs and get ready. Put on your prettiest dresses, because there's going to be dancing. When it's time, I'll come by for you."

Dancing?

Adrenalin surged through Dottie's body at the thought of getting that close to him. Heat poured off her, but she couldn't attribute all of it to the sun. She suspected his announcement had caused a spike in her temperature.

Her mind went through a mental search of her wardrobe. The only thing possibly presentable for such an affair was her simple black dress with her black high heels.

"Will it be a large party, Your Highness?"

He darted her a curious glance. "Thirty or so guests, mostly family friends. If you're both finished with dinner, let's go upstairs."

After gathering their things, Dottie said she'd see them later and she hurried back to her bedroom for a long shower and shampoo. She blowdried her hair and left it loose with a side part, then put on her black dress with the cap sleeves and round neck.

While she was applying her coral-frost lipstick, she thought she heard a noise in the other room. When she went to investigate, she saw Zoe looking like a vision in a long white dress with ruffles and a big yellow sash. But her face was awash in tears. She came running to her.

Without conscious thought, Dottie knelt down and

drew her into her arms. It was the first hug she'd given her, but she could no longer hold back. Zoe clung to her while she wept, exactly the way Cory had done so many hundreds of times when he'd needed comfort.

"What's wrong, darling?"

"Daddy's going to get married."

Dottie was trying to understand. "Don't you mean your uncle?"

"No—I heard *Yiayia* tell Sofia. My daddy's going to marry Princess Genevieve. But I want *you* to be my new mommy. When I kissed *Yiayia* good-night, she told me Princess Genevieve will be at the party and I had to be good."

A stabbing pain attacked Dottie until she could hardly breathe. "I see. Zoe, this is something you need to talk to your daddy about, but not until you go to bed. Does he know you're here with me?"

"No."

Dottie stood up. "I need to phone Hector so he can tell your daddy you ran to my room."

When that was done, she took Zoe in the bathroom. After wetting a washcloth, she wiped the tears off her face. "There. Now we're ready. When we get to the party, I want you to smile and keep smiling. Can you do that for me?"

After a slight hesitation, Zoe nodded.

Dottie clasped her hand and walked her back in the other room. "Have I told you how pretty you look in your new dress?"

"Both of you look absolutely beautiful," came the sound of a deep, familiar voice.

Alex.

Dottie gasped softly when she saw that he'd entered

the room. Since Zoe had left the door open, he must not have felt the need to knock. The prince, tall and dark, had dressed in a formal, midnight-blue suit and tie, taking her breath. His penetrating black eyes swept over her, missing nothing. The look in them sent a river of heat through her body.

"Zoe wanted to show me how she looked, Your Highness. In her haste, she forgot to tell Sofia."

He looked so handsome when he smiled, Dottie felt light-headed. "That's understandable. This is my daughter's first real party. Are you ready?"

When Zoe nodded, he grasped her other hand and the three of them left the room. He led them down the grand staircase where they could hear music and voices. Though Zoe lacked her usual sparkle, she kept smiling like the princess she was. Her training had served her well. Even at her young age, she moved with the grace and dignity of a royal.

Some of the elegantly dressed guests were dancing, others were eating. The three of them passed through a receiving line of titled people and close friends of the Constantinides family.

"Zoe?" her father said. "I'd like you to meet Princess Genevieve."

For a minute, Dottie reeled. She'd seen the lovely young princess in the news. Zoe was a trooper and handled their first meeting beautifully. One royal princess to another. Dottie loved Zoe for her great show of poise in front of the woman she didn't want for her new mother.

Dottie was trying to see the good. It was natural that Alex would marry again, and Zoe desperately needed a mother's love. Plus their match would give Alex more children and Zoe wouldn't have to be the only child. In that respect it was more necessary than ever that her speech improve enough that when Alex married Princess Genevieve, his daughter could make herself understood. Zoe also needed to be strong in her English speech because she would be tested when French was introduced into their household. Princess Genevieve would expect it. The House of Helvetia was located on the south side of Lake Geneva in the French-speaking region.

Now that she knew of Alex's future plans, Dottie had to focus on the additional goal to pursue for his daughter. She needed to help prepare Zoe for the next phase in her life and—

"My, my. What have we here?"

A male voice Dottie didn't recognize broke in on her thoughts. She turned her head to discover another extremely attractive man with black hair standing at the end of the line. Almost the same height as Alex, he bore a superficial resemblance to him, but his features were less rugged. The brothers could be the same age, which she estimated to be early to mid-thirties.

When she realized it was Crown Prince Stasio, she curtsied. "Welcome home, Your Highness."

He flashed her an infectious smile. "You don't need to do that around me. My little brother told me you're working with Zoe. That makes us all family. Did anyone ever tell you you're very easy on the eyes?" His were black, too. "Alex held back on that pertinent fact."

What a tease he was! "Zoe told me you were funny. I think she's right."

The crown prince laughed. She noticed he had a fabulous tan. "Tell me about yourself. Where have you been hiding all my life?" He was incorrigible and so different from Alex, who was more serious minded. Of the two, Dottie privately thought that Zoe's father seemed much more the natural ruler of their country.

"I'm from New York."

His eyes narrowed. "Coming to Hellenica must feel like you dropped off the edge of the planet, right?"

"It's paradise here."

"It is now that I've got my little Zoe to dance with." He reached over and picked up his niece. After they hugged, he set her down again. "Come on. I'm going to spin you around the ballroom."

Zoe's smile lit up for real as he whirled her away. Dancing lessons hadn't been wasted on her either. She moved like a royal princess who was years older, capturing everyone's attention. People started clapping. Dottie couldn't have been prouder of her if she'd been Zoe's real mother.

While she watched, she felt a strong hand slip around her waist. The next thing she knew Alex had drawn her into his arms. His wonderful, clean male scent and the brush of his legs against hers sent sparks of electricity through her system. In her heels, she was a little taller and felt like their bodies had been made for each other.

"Why won't you look at me?" he whispered. "Everyone's going to think you don't like me."

"I'm trying to concentrate on our dancing. It's been a long time." The soft rock had a hypnotizing effect on her. She could stay like this for hours, almost but not quite embracing him.

"For me, too. I've been waiting ages to get you in my arms like this. If it's in plain sight of our guests, so be it. You feel good to me, Dottie. So damn good you're in danger of being carried off. Only my princely duty keeps me from doing what I feel like doing."

Ah… Before Zoe's revelations in the bedroom tonight, Dottie might have allowed herself to be carried away. The clamorings of her body had come to painful life and only he could assuage them.

"I understand. That's why I'm going to say goodnight after this dance. There are other female guests in the ballroom no doubt waiting for their turn around the floor with you. You're a terrific dancer, by the way."

"There's only one woman I want to be with tonight and she's right here within kissing distance. You could have no idea the willpower it's taking not to taste that tempting mouth of yours." He spoke with an intensity that made her legs go weak. "While we were out at the pool, I would have pulled you in if Zoe hadn't been with us."

"It's a good thing you didn't. Otherwise your daughter will be more confused than ever when she sees you ask Princess Genevieve to dance."

His body stiffened. She'd hit a nerve, but he had no clue it had pierced her to the depths. "I know you well enough to realize you had a deliberate reason for bringing up her name. Why did you do it?"

Dottie's heart died a little because the music had stopped, bringing those thrilling moments in his arms to an end. She lifted her head and looked at him for the first time since they'd entered the ballroom. "When you put Zoe to bed tonight, she'll tell you. Thank you for an enchanting evening, Your Highness. I won't forget. See you in the morning."

She eased out of his arms and walked out of the

ballroom. But the second she reached the staircase, she raced up the steps and ran the rest of the way to her room.

"Dot," Zoe called to her the next morning as she and her father came into the classroom. "Look at this?" She held up a CD.

"What's on it?"

"It's a surprise. Put it in your laptop," said Alex.

After giving him a curious glance, Dottie walked around to the end of the table and put it in. After a moment they could all see last night's events at the party on the screen, complete with the music. There she was enclosed in Alex's arms. Princess Genevieve would not have been happy.

Whoever had taken the video had caught everything, including what went on after Dottie had left the ballroom. Her throat swelled with emotion as she watched Alex dance with his daughter. If he'd asked Princess Genevieve to dance, that portion hadn't been put on the CD.

She smiled at Zoe. "You're so lucky to have a video of your first party. Did you love it?"

"Yes!" There weren't any shadows in the little girl's eyes. Whatever conversation had taken place between father and daughter at bedtime, she looked happy. "Uncle Stasi told me I could stand on his feet while he danced with me. He made me laugh."

"The crown prince is a real character." Her gaze swerved to Alex. "He made me laugh, as well. I've decided you and your brother must have given certain people some nervous moments when you were younger."

Alex's grin turned her heart right over. "Our parents

particularly. My brother was upset you left the party before he could dance with you."

"Maybe that was for the best. My high heels might have hurt the tops of his feet."

At that remark both he and Zoe laughed. Dottie was enjoying this too much and suggested they get started on the morning lesson.

They worked in harmony until Alex said it was time for lunch by the pool. After they'd finished eating, Zoe ran into the cabana to get into her swimsuit. Dottie took advantage of the time they were alone to talk to him.

"I'm glad we're by ourselves for a minute. I want to discuss Zoe's preschool situation and wondered how you'd feel if I went with her to class in the morning. You know, just to prop up her confidence. We'll come back here for lunch and enjoy our afternoon session with her out here. What do you think?"

He sipped his coffee. "That's an excellent suggestion. Otherwise she'll keep putting off wanting to go back."

"Exactly."

Alex released a sigh. "Since our talk about her friends, I've worried about her being away from the other children this long."

Dottie was glad they were on her same wavelength. "Is there any particular child she's close to at school?"

Their gazes held. "Not that she has mentioned. As you know, school hasn't been her best experience."

"Then tell me this. Who goes to the school?"

"Besides those who live in Hellenica, there are a few children of some younger diplomats who attend at the various elementary grade levels."

"From where?"

"The U.K., France, Italy, Bosnia, Germany, the States."

The States? "That's interesting." Dottie started to get excited, but she kept her ideas to herself and finished her coffee.

Alex didn't say anything more, yet she felt a strange new tension growing between them. Her awareness of him was so powerful, she couldn't sit there any longer. "If you'll excuse me, I'll go change into my bathing suit."

"Not yet," he countered. "There's something I need to tell you before Zoe comes out."

Her pulse picked up speed. "If it's about her running to my room last eve—"

"It is," he cut in on her. "After what Zoe told me while I was putting her to bed, I realize this matter needs to be cleared up."

"Your marriage to Princess Genevieve is none of my business. As long as—"

"Dottie," he interrupted her again, this time with an underlying trace of impatience. "There will be no marriage. Believe me when I tell you there was never any question of my marrying her. I impressed that on Zoe before she went to sleep."

Dottie had to fight to prevent Alex from seeing her great relief and joy.

"Since Teresa's death, it has been my grandmother's ambition to join the House of Helvetia to our own. Zoe had the great misfortune of overhearing her tell Sofia about her plans. In her innocence, Zoe has expressed her love for you and has told *Yiayia* she wants *you* to be her new mommy."

"I was afraid of that," she whispered.

"Last night I spoke to my grandmother. She admitted that she arranged last night's party for me, not Stasi. She hoped that by inviting Princess Genevieve, it would put an end to Zoe's foolishness."

"Oh, dear."

"The queen has taken great pains to remind me once again what a wonderful mother Teresa was and that it is time I took another wife. Naturally she's grateful you've identified Zoe's problem, but now she wants you to go back to New York. I learned she's already found another speech therapist to replace you."

Dottie's head reared. "Who?"

"I have no idea, but it's not important. My grandmother is running true to form," he said before Dottie could comment further. "She tried to use all her logic with me by reminding me Zoe will have to be taken care of by a nanny until maturity; therefore it won't be good to allow her to get any more attached to you."

"In that regard, she's right."

Anger rose inside him. "Nevertheless, the queen stepped way out of bounds last night. I told her that I had no plans to marry again. She would have to find another way to strengthen the ties with Helvetia because Zoe's welfare was my only concern and you were staying put."

His dark eyes pierced hers. "I'm sure my words have shocked you, but it's necessary you know the truth so there won't be any more misunderstandings."

"Daddy?" They both turned to see Zoe trying to drag out her five-foot inflated whale from the cabana, but it was stuck. "I need help!"

Before he moved in her direction he said, "My grandmother may still be the ruler of Hellenica, but I rule over my own life and Zoe's. My daughter knows she doesn't have to worry about Princess Genevieve ever again, no matter what her *yiayia* might say."

With that declaration, he took a few steps, then paused. "Just so you know, after I've put Zoe to bed tonight, I'm taking you to the old part of the city, so don't plan on an early night."

Alex stayed with Zoe and read stories to her until she fell asleep. Since she realized he wasn't going to marry Princess Genevieve, his daughter actually seemed at peace for a change. With a nod to Sofia in the next room to keep an eye on her, he left for his own suite.

He showered and shaved before dressing in a sport shirt and trousers. On his way out of the room, he called for an unmarked car with smoked glass to be brought around to his private entrance. With Stasio in the palace, Alex didn't need to worry about anything else tonight. He called security and asked them to escort Dottie to the entrance.

After she climbed in the back with him, he explained that they were driving to the city's ancient amphitheater to see the famous sound and light show. "We're going to visit the site of many archaeological ruins. As we walk around, you'll see evidence of the Cycladic civilization and the Byzantium empire."

Alex had seen the show many times before with visiting dignitaries, but tonight he was with Dottie and he'd never felt so alive. The balmy air caused him to forget everything but the exciting woman who sat next to him.

Throughout the program he could tell by her questions and remarks that she loved it. After it was over he lounged against a temple column while she explored.

The tourists had started leaving, yet all he could see was her beautiful silhouette against the night sky. She'd put her hair back so her distinctive profile was revealed. She was dressed in another skirt and blouse, and he was reminded of the first time he'd seen her in his office.

"Dottie?" he called softly in the fragrant night air as he moved behind her. She let out a slight gasp and swung around.

He caught her to him swiftly and kissed her mouth to stop any other sound from escaping. Her lips were warm and tempting, but he didn't deepen the kiss. "Forgive me for doing that," he whispered against them, "but I didn't want you to say *Your Highness* and draw attention. Come and get in the car. It's late."

He helped her into the backseat with him and shut the door. "I'm not going to apologize for what I did," he murmured against her hot cheek. "If you want to slap me, you have my permission. But if I'm going to be punished for it, I'll take my chances now and give you a proper reason."

Alex's compelling mouth closed over Dottie's with a hunger that set her knees knocking. She'd sensed this moment was inevitable. Since her arrival in Hellenica, they'd been together early in the morning, late at night and most of the hours in between. He possessed a lethal sensuality for which she had no immunity.

Knowing he had no plans to marry Princess Genevieve, Dottie settled deeper into his arms and found herself giving him kiss for kiss. It was time she faced an ironic truth about herself. She wasn't any different than the rest of the female population who found the prince so attractive, they'd give anything to be in her position.

Royal scandal might abound, but she'd just discovered there was a reason for it. Forbidden fruit with this gorgeous male made these moments of physical intimacy exquisite. When a man was as incredibly potent and exciting as Alex, you could blot out everything else, even the fact that the driver ferrying them back to the palace was aware of every sound of ecstasy pouring out of her.

She finally put her hands against his chest and tore her mouth from his so she could ease back enough to look at him. Still trying to catch her breath, she asked, "Do you know what we are, Your Highness?" Her voice sounded less than steady to her own ears. She hated her inability to control that part of her.

"Suppose you tell me," he said in a husky voice.

"We're both a cliché. The prince and the hired help, nipping out for a little pleasure. I've just confirmed everything I've ever read in books and have seen on the news about palace intrigue."

"Who are you more angry at?" he murmured, kissing the tips of her fingers. "Me, for having taken unfair advantage? Or you, for having the right of refusal at any time which you didn't exercise? I'm asking myself if I'm fighting your righteous indignation that served you too late, or the ghost of your dead husband."

She squirmed because he'd hit the mark dead center. "Both," she answered honestly.

"Tell me about your husband. Was it love at first sight with him?"

"I don't know. It just seemed right from the beginning."

"Give me a few details. I really want to know what it would be like to have that kind of freedom."

Dottie stirred restlessly, sensing he meant what he said. "We met in Albany, New York, where I was raised. I went to the local pharmacy to pick up a prescription for my aunt. Neil had just been hired as a new pharmacist. It was late and there weren't any other customers.

"He told me it would take a while to get it ready, so we began talking. The next day he phoned and asked me out with the excuse that he'd just moved there from New York City and didn't know anyone. He was fun and kind and very smart.

"On our first date we went to a movie. After it was over, he told me he was going to marry me and there was nothing I could do about it. Four months later we got married and before we knew it, Cory was on the way. I was incredibly happy."

Alex's arm tightened around her. "I envy you for having those kinds of memories."

"Surely you have some wonderful ones, too."

A troubled sigh escaped his lips. "To quote you on several occasions, even if I am a prince, the one thing I've never had power over was my own personal happiness. Duty to my country came first. My marriage to Teresa was planned years before we got together, so any relationships I had before the wedding couldn't be taken seriously.

"She was beautiful in her own way, very accomplished. Sweet. But it was never an affair of the heart or anything close to it. On his deathbed, my father commanded me to marry her. I couldn't tell him I wouldn't."

Dottie shuddered. "Did you love him?"

"Yes."

"I can't comprehend being in your shoes, but I

admire you for being so devoted to your father and your country. Did Teresa love you?"

He took a steadying breath. "Before she died, she told me she'd fallen in love with me. I told her the same thing, not wanting to hurt her. She told me I was a liar, but she said she loved me for it."

"Oh, Alex… How hard for both of you."

"I wanted to fall in love with her, but we both know you can't force something that's not there. Zoe was my one gift from the gods who brood over Mount Pelos."

Her gaze lifted to his. "Not to be in love and have to marry—that's anathema to me. No wonder you seek relief in the shadows with someone handy like me. I get it, Alex. I really do. And you *didn't* take unfair advantage of me. It's been so long since I've been around an attractive man, my hormones are out of kilter right now."

"Is that what this tension is between us? Hormones?" he said with a twinge of bitterness she felt pierce her where it hurt most.

"I don't have a better word for it." She buried her face in her hands. "I loved Neil more than you can imagine. Thank heaven neither of us had a royal bone in our bodies to prevent us from knowing joy."

He stroked the back of her neck in a way that sent fingers of delight down her spine. "How did you manage after they were killed?"

"My aunt. She reminded me not everyone had been as lucky as I'd been. Her boyfriend got killed when he was deployed overseas in the military, so she never married. In her inimitable way she told me to stop pitying myself and get on with something useful.

"Her advice prompted me to go to graduate school

in New York City and become a speech therapist. After graduation I was hired on by the Stillman Institute. Little did I know that all the time I'd been helping Cory with his speech that last year, I was preparing for a lifetime career."

"Is your aunt still alive?"

"No. She died fourteen months ago."

"I'm sorry. I wish she were still living so I could thank her for her inspired advice. My Zoe is thriving because of you." He pulled her closer. "What about your parents?"

"They died in a car crash when I was just a little girl."

"It saddens me you've had to deal with so much grief."

"It comes to us all. In my aunt's case, it was good she passed away. With her chronic pneumonia, she could never recover and every illness made her worse."

"My mother was like that. She had been so ill that Stasi and I were thankful once she took her last breath."

"What about your father?"

"He developed an aggressive cancer of the thyroid. After he was gone, my grandmother took over to make sure we were raised according to her exacting Valleder standards. She was the power behind my grandfather's throne."

"She's done a wonderful job. I'll tell her that when I leave Hellenica." Dottie took a deep breath and sat back in the seat. "And now, despite her disapproval that I haven't left yet, here I am making out in an unmarked car with Prince Alexius Constantinides. How *could* you have given Zoe such an impossible last name? Nine consonants. *Nine!* And two of them are *T*'s," she half sobbed as the dam broke and she felt tears on her cheeks.

Alex reached over and smoothed the moisture from her face. He put his lips where his hand had been. "I'm glad there are nine. I won't let you go until she can pronounce our last name perfectly. That's going to take a long time."

"You'll have gone through at least half a dozen speech therapists by then."

"Possibly, but you'll be there in the background until she no longer needs your services."

"We've been over this ground before."

"We haven't even started," he declared as if announcing an edict. "Shall we get out of the car? We've been back at the palace for the past ten minutes. My driver probably wants to go to bed, which is where we should be."

She didn't think he meant that the way it came out, but with Alex you couldn't be absolutely sure when his teasing side would suddenly show up. All she knew was that her face was suffused with heat. She flung the car door open and ran into the palace, leaving him in the proverbial royal dust.

The death of her husband had put an end to all fairy tales, and that was the only place a prince could stay. She refused to be in the background of his life. It was time to close the storybook for good.

CHAPTER SIX

AT ELEVEN-FORTY-FIVE the next morning, Alex did something unprecedented and drove to the preschool to pick up Zoe and Dottie himself. He'd decided he'd better wear something more formal for this public visit and chose his dove-grey suit with a white shirt and grey vest. He toned it with a darker grey tie that bore the royal crest of the monarchy in silver, wanting to look his best for the woman who'd already turned his world inside out.

The directress of the school accompanied him to the classroom, where he spotted his daughter sitting in front and Dottie seated in the back. As the woman announced the arrival of Prince Alexius Constantinides, Dottie's blue eyes widened in shock. Her gaze clung to his for a moment.

He heard a collective sound of awe from the children, something he was used to in his capacity as prince. Children were always a delight. He was enjoying this immensely, but it was clear Dottie was stunned that he'd decided to come and get them. He knew in his gut her eyes wouldn't have ignited like that if she hadn't been happy to see him.

The teacher, Mrs. Pappas, urged the roomful of

twelve children to stand and bow. Zoe stood up, but she turned and smiled at Dottie before saying good morning to His Royal Highness along with the others. Alex got a kick out of the whole thing as the children kept looking at Zoe, knowing he was her daddy.

He'd never seen his daughter this happy in his life, and he should have done this before now. It lit up her whole being. Dottie was transforming his life in whole new ways. Because of her influence, Alex wanted to give his struggling preschooler a needed boost this morning. But she wasn't so struggling now that she had Dottie in her court.

He shook hands with everyone, then they returned to the palace. After changing into his swimming trunks, he joined them at the pool for lunch. With Zoe running around, he could finally talk to Dottie in private.

"How did my daughter do in class?"

"She participated without hanging back."

"That's because you've given her the confidence."

"You know it's been a team effort. While I've got you alone for a minute, let me tell you something else that happened this morning."

Alex could tell she was excited. "Go ahead."

"I arranged to talk with the directress about Zoe and was given permission to visit the other preschool class. One of the boys enrolled is an American from Pennsylvania named Mark Varney. He's supposed to be in first grade, but his parents put him back in preschool because he has no knowledge of Greek and needs to start with the basics. The situation has made him un-happy and he's turning into a loner."

"And you've decided that two negatives could make a positive?"

"Maybe." She half laughed. "It's scary how well you read my mind. Here's the thing—if you sanctioned it and Mark's parents allowed him to come back to the palace after school next time, he and Zoe could have some one-on-one time here in the pool, or down on the beach. I'd help them with their lessons, but the rest of the time they could have fun together. A play date is what she needs."

"I couldn't agree more."

"Oh, good! The directress says he's feeling inadequate. If his parents understood the circumstances and explained to him about Zoe's speech problem, he might be willing to help her and they could become friends in the process. That would help his confidence level, too."

Alex heard the appeal in Dottie's voice. "I'll ask Hector to handle it and we'll see how the first play date goes."

Light filled her blue eyes, dazzling him. "Thank you for being willing."

"That's rather ironic for you to be thanking me. I'm the one who should be down on my knees to you for thinking of it. She's a different child already because of you."

"You keep saying that, but you don't give yourself enough credit, Alex. When she saw you walk into the schoolroom earlier today, her heart was in her eyes. I wish I'd had a camera on me so I could have taken a picture. Every father should have a daughter who loves him that much. The extra time you've spent with her lately is paying huge dividends. I know it's taking time away from your duties, but if you can keep it up, you'll never regret it."

He rubbed his lower lip with the pad of his thumb,

staring at her through shuttered eyes. "That's why I sent for Stasi to come home. With you showing me the way, I'm well aware Zoe needs me and am doing everything in my power to free myself up."

"I know." She suddenly broke away from his gaze to look at Zoe. "She's waiting for us. Today we'll work on the letter *C*. Her preschool teacher brought her own cat to class. The children learned how to take care of one. Zoe got to pet it and couldn't have been more thrilled."

Dottie had inexplicably changed the subject and was talking faster than usual, a sign that something was going on inside her, making her uncomfortable. When she got up from the chair, he followed her over to the edge of the pool and listened as she engaged his daughter in a conversation that was really a teaching moment. She had a remarkable, unique way of communicating. Zoe ate it up. Why wouldn't she? There was no one else like Dottie.

Dottie was more than a speech therapist for his daughter. She was her advocate. Her selfless efforts to help Zoe lead a normal life couldn't be repaid with gifts or perks or money she'd already refused to accept. The woman wanted his daughter to succeed for the purest of reasons. She wanted it for a stranger's child, too. That made Dottie Richards a person of interest to him in ways that went deep beneath the surface.

Alex took off his sandals and dove into the deep end. After doing some underwater laps, he emerged next to his daughter, causing her to shriek with laughter. The day had been idyllic and it wasn't over.

As he did more laps, his thoughts drifted to his conversation with Dottie last night. When he'd turned eighteen, his family had arranged the betrothal to Princess

Teresa. However, until he'd been ready to commit to marriage, he'd known pleasure and desire with various women over the years. Those women had understood nothing long lasting could come of the relationship. No one woman's memory had lingered long in his mind. Forget his heart.

When Zoe came along, their daughter gave them both something new and wonderful to focus on. With Teresa's passing, Zoe had become the joy of his life. There'd been other women in the past two years, but the part of his psyche that had never been touched was still a void.

Enter Dottie Richards, a woman who'd buried a son and husband. He could still hear her saying she'd lost the great loves of her life. She'd experienced the kind of overwhelming love denied him because of his royal roots. He really envied her the freedom to choose the man who'd satisfied her passion at its deepest level and had given her a child.

Though it was an unworthy sentiment, Alex found himself resenting her husband for that same freedom. If Alex had been a commoner and had met her in his early twenties—before she'd met her husband—would she have been as attracted to him as he was to her? Would they have married?

She wasn't indifferent to Alex. The way she'd kissed him back last night convinced him of her strong attraction to him. He'd also sensed her interest at odd times when he noticed her eyes on him. The way she sometimes breathed faster around him for no apparent reason. But he had no way to gauge the true depth of her emotions until he could get her alone again.

As for his feelings, all he knew was that she'd lit a

fire inside him. In two weeks, even without physical intimacy, Dottie affected him more than Teresa had ever done during the three years of their marriage.

For the first time in his life he was suddenly waking up every morning hardly able to breathe until he saw her. For the only time in his existence he was questioning everything about the royal legacy that made him who he was and dictated his destiny.

His jealousy terrified him. He'd seen his brother's interest in her. Stasi's arranged marriage would be happening on his thirty-fifth birthday, in less than three weeks now. Until then it didn't stop him from enjoying and looking at other women. But it had angered Alex, who felt territorial when it came to Dottie. That's why he hadn't let Stasi dance with her. Alex had no right to feel this way, but the situation had gone way beyond rights.

Alex *wanted* his daughter's speech therapist. But as he'd already learned, a command from him meant nothing to her. A way had to be found so she wouldn't leave, but he had to be careful that he didn't frighten her off.

He swam back to Zoe, who hung on to the edge of the pool, practicing the hard *C* sound with Dottie. Without looking him in the eye, Dottie said, "Here's your daddy. Now that your lesson is over, I have to go inside. Zoe, I need to tell you now that I won't be able come to your bedroom to say good-night later. I have plans I can't break, but I'll see you in the morning." She finally glanced at him. "Your Highness."

Alex had no doubts that if she'd dared and if it wouldn't have alarmed Zoe, Dottie would have run away from him as fast as she could. Fortunately one of the positive benefits of being the prince meant he could keep twenty-four-hour surveillance on her.

After she'd left the sun deck, he spent another half hour in the pool with his daughter before they went inside. But once in her room, Zoe told Sofia to go away. When Alex tried to reason with her and get her to apologize, she broke down in tears, begging him to eat dinner with her in her room. She didn't want to be with *Yiayia*.

Dottie's announcement that she wouldn't be coming in to say good-night had sent the sun behind a black cloud. Naturally Dottie had every right to spend her evenings the way she wished. That's what he told Zoe. He had to help his daughter see that, but the idyllic day had suddenly vanished like a curl of smoke in the air.

"Make her come, Daddy."

A harsh laugh escaped his lips. You didn't make Dottie do anything. He didn't have that kind of power. She had to do it herself because she wanted to.

What if she *didn't* want to? What if the memory of life with her husband trapped her in the past and she couldn't, or didn't want to, reach out? On the heels of those questions came an even more important one.

Why would she reach out? What did a prince have to offer a commoner? An affair? A secret life? The answers to that question not only stared him in the face, they kicked him in the gut with enough violence to knock the wind out of him.

Once Zoe was asleep, Alex left for his suite, taking the palace stairs three steps at a time to the next floor. The last person he expected to find in his living room was Stasio with a glass of scotch in his hand.

He tossed back a drink. "It's about time you made an appearance, little brother." For a while now a cross-grain tone of discontent had lain behind Stasi's speech and it had grown stronger over the last few months. No crystal ball was needed here. The bitter subject of arranged marriages still burned like acid on his tongue as it did on Stasi's.

"Did you and *Yiayia* have another row tonight?" Alex started unbuttoning his shirt and took off his shoes.

"What do you mean, another one?" Stasio slammed his half-empty glass on the coffee table, spilling some of it. "It's been the same argument for seventeen years, but tonight I put an end to it."

"Translate for me," Alex rapped out tersely.

Stasio's mouth thinned to a white line. "I told her I broke it off with Beatriz while I was in Valleder. I can't go through with the wedding."

Alex felt the hairs on the back of his neck stand on end. He stared hard at his brother. All the time Stasi had put off coming home, something in the back of Alex's mind had divined the truth, but he hadn't been able to make his brother open up about it.

Since Stasio had been old enough to comprehend life, he'd been forced to bear the burden of knowing he would be king one day. That was hard enough. But to be married for the rest of his life to a woman he didn't love would have kept him in a living hell. No one knew it better than Alex.

"How is Beatriz dealing with it?"

"Not well," he whispered in agony.

"But she's always known how you truly felt. No matter how much this has hurt her, deep down it couldn't have come as a complete surprise. I thought she would have broken it off a long time ago."

"That miracle never happened. She wanted the marriage, just the way Teresa wanted yours." Alex couldn't deny it. "What always astounded me was that you were able to handle going through with your marriage to her."

Alex wheeled around. "The truth?"

"Always."

"It was the last thing I wanted. I wouldn't have married her, but with Father on his deathbed making me promise to follow through with it, I couldn't take the fight with him any longer and caved. The only thing that kept me sane was the fact that I wouldn't be king one day, so I wouldn't have to be in the public eye every second. And then, Zoe came along. Now I can't imagine my life without her."

Stasio paled. "Neither can I. She's the one ray of sunshine around this tomb." He took a deep breath. "Under the circumstances I should be grateful *Yiayia* isn't taking her last breath because there will be no forced wedding with Beatriz. Philippe has backed me in this and he holds a certain sway with our grandmother."

Alex was afraid that was wishful thinking on Stasio's part. Not only was Philippe his best friend, he'd been one of the lucky royals who'd ended up marrying the American girl he'd loved years earlier. They'd had a son together and the strict rules had been waived in his particular case.

But the queen hadn't approved of Philippe's marriage, so it didn't follow she would give an inch when it came to Stasio's decision. In her eyes he'd created a monumental catastrophe that could never be forgiven.

"So what's going to happen now?"

"Beatriz's parents have given a statement to the press. It's probably all over the news as we speak or will be in a matter of hours. Once the story grows legs, I'll be torn apart. I had to tell *Yiayia* tonight to prepare her for what's coming."

"What was our grandmother's reaction?"

"You know her as well as I do. Putting on her stone face, she said the coronation would go ahead as scheduled to save the integrity of the crown. A suitable marriage with another princess will take place within six months maximum. She gave me her short list of five candidates."

Alex felt a chill go through him. "Putting the cart before the horse has never been done."

"The queen is going to have her way no matter what. Let's face it. She's not well and wants me to take over."

"Stasi—"

Sick for his brother, he walked over and hugged him. "I'm here for you always. You know that."

"I *do*. A fine pair we've turned out to be. She told me you're still resisting marriage to Princess Genevieve."

"Like you, I told her no once and for all," he said through clenched teeth. "I sacrificed myself once. Never again."

"She's not going to give up on Genevieve. I heard it in her voice."

"That's too bad because my only duty now is to raise Zoe to be happy."

With the help of Dottie, he intended that to become a reality. Walking over to the table, he poured himself a drink. He lifted his glass to his brother.

"To you, Stasi," he said in a thick-toned voice. "May God help you find a way to cope." *May God help both of us.*

* * *

After a sleep troubled with thoughts of Alex, Dottie felt out of sorts and anxious and only poked at her breakfast. Since he hadn't brought Zoe for her morning session yet, she checked her emails. Among some posts from her friends at the Institute in New York she'd received a response to the email she'd sent Dr. Rice. With a pounding heart, she opened it first.

Dear Dottie:

Thank you for giving me an update on Princess Zoe. I'm very pleased to hear that she's beginning to make progress. If anyone can work miracles, it's you. In reference to your request, I've interviewed several therapists who I believe would work well with her, but the one I think could be the best fit might not be available as soon as you wanted. She's still working with the parent of another child to teach them coaching skills. I'll let you know when she'll be free to come. Give it a few more days.

By the way, it's all over the news about Crown Prince Stasio calling off his wedding to Princess Beatriz. She's here in Manhattan. I saw her on the news walking into the St. Regis Hotel. What a coincidence that you're working for Prince Alexius. Have you ever met his brother? Well, take care. I'll be in touch before long. Dr. Rice.

She rested her elbow on the table, covering her eyes with her hand. Prince Stasio's teasing facade hid a courageous man who'd just done himself and Princess Beatriz a huge favor, even if talk of it and the judgments that would follow saturated the news.

The world had no idea what went on behind the closed doors of a desperately unhappy couple, royal or otherwise. What woman or man would want to be married to someone who'd been chosen for them years earlier? Alex's first marriage had been forced. It boggled the mind, yet it had happened to the royals of the Constantinides family for hundreds of years in order to keep the monarchy alive.

Poor Zoe. To think that dear little girl would have to grow up knowing an arranged marriage was her fate. Dottie cringed at the prospect. Surely Alex wouldn't do that to his own daughter after what he and his brother had been through, would he?

"Dot?" Zoe came running into the alcove and hugged her so hard, she almost fell off the chair.

Without conscious thought Dottie closed her eyes and hugged her back, aching for this family and its archaic rules that had hung like a pall over their lives. When she opened them again, there was Alex standing there in a navy crew neck and jeans looking bigger than life as he watched the two of them interact.

She saw lines and shadows on his striking face that hadn't been there yesterday. But when their eyes met, the black fire in his took her to the backseat of the car where the other night they'd kissed each other with mindless abandon.

"We're here to invite you out for a day on the water," he explained. "The galley's loaded with food and drink. We'll do lessons and have fun at the same time."

As he spoke, Zoe sat down to do one of the puzzles on the table out of hearing distance. It was a good thing, because Alex's invitation had frightened Dottie. Though her mind was warning her this would be a mistake, that vital organ pumping her life's blood enlarged at the prospect.

The other night she'd almost lost control with him and the experience was still too fresh. To go with him would be like watching a moth enticed to a flame fly straight to its death.

"Perhaps it's time you enjoyed one day without me along. It won't hurt Zoe to miss a lesson." She'd said the first thing to come into her mind, frantically searching for an excuse not to be with him.

Lines marred his arresting features. "I'm afraid this is one time I need your cooperation. There's something critically urgent I must discuss with you."

Dottie looked away from the intensity of his gaze. This had to be about his brother. The distinct possibility that Prince Stasio needed Alex to do double duty for him right now, or to spend more time with him, crossed her mind. Of necessity it would cut short the time he'd been spending with Zoe. If that was the case, she could hardly turn him down while he worked out an alternative plan with her.

"All right. Give me a minute to put some things in the bag for our lesson."

"Take all the time you need." His voice seemed to have a deeper timbre this morning, playing havoc with the butterflies fluttering madly in her chest.

After Zoe helped pack some things they'd need, Dottie changed into a sleeveless top and shorts. When she emerged from the bathroom with her hair freshly brushed, the prince took swift inventory of her face and figure, whipping up a storm of heat that stained her cheeks with color. Once she'd stowed her swimsuit in the bag, she put on her sunglasses and declared she was ready to go.

Dottie had assumed they'd be taking his sailboat. But once they left the palace grounds, Alex informed her he had business on one of the other islands so they were going out on the yacht. The news caused a secret thrill to permeate her body.

That first morning when she and Zoe had gone down to the private beach, she'd seen the gleaming white royal yacht moored in the distance. Like any normal tourist, she'd dreamed of touring the Aegean on a boat while she was in Hellenica. Today the dream had become reality as she boarded the fabulous luxury craft containing every amenity known to man.

With the sparkling blue water so calm, Zoe was in heaven. Wearing another swimsuit, this one in lime-and-blue stripes, she ran up and down the length of it with her father's binoculars, looking for groupers and parrot fish with one of the crew.

Alex settled them in side-by-side loungers while the deck steward placed drinks and treats close enough to reach. With Zoe occupied for a few minutes, Dottie felt this would be the best time to approach him about his brother and turned in his direction. But he'd removed his shirt. One look at his chest with its dusting of black hair, in fact his entire masculine physique, and she had to stifle a moan.

The other night she'd been crushed against him and, heaven help her, she longed to repeat the experience. Fortunately the presence of Zoe and the crew prevented anything like that from happening today.

Admit you want it to happen, Dottie.

After losing Neil, she couldn't believe all these feelings to know a man's possession had come back this strongly. For so long she'd been dead inside. She was frightened by this explosion of need Alex had ignited. She had to hope Dr. Rice would email her the good news that her replacement could be here by next week because she could feel herself being sucked into a situation that could only rebound on her.

Not for a moment did she believe Alex was a womanizer. He was a man, and like any single male was free to find temporary satisfaction with a willing woman when the time and opportunity presented itself. With her full cooperation he'd acted on one of those opportunities and she'd lost her head.

It wasn't his fault. It was *hers*. She'd been an idiot.

Unless she wanted a new form of heartache to plague her for the rest of her life, she couldn't afford another foolish moment because of overwhelming desire for Alex. There was no future in it. She'd be gone from this assignment before long. Nothing but pain could come from indulging in a passionate interlude with a prince. *Nothing.*

"Alex. The head of my department at Stillman's responded to one of my emails this morning."

He removed his sunglasses and shifted his hard-muscled body on the lounger so he faced her. "Was that the one asking him to find another therapist for Zoe?" he inquired in a dangerously silky voice. An underlying tone of ice sent a tremor through her body.

"Yes. He says he'll probably have someone to replace me within another week. By then Zoe ought to have more confidence in herself and will work well with the new speech teacher."

Paralyzing tension stretched between them before

eyes of jet impaled her. "You don't believe that piece of fiction any more than I do. In any event, there can't be a question about you leaving, not with the coronation almost upon us."

She sat up in surprise. "You mean there's still going to be one?"

Like lightning he levered himself from the lounger. "Why would you ask that question?"

"At the end of Dr. Rice's email, he told me there were headlines about Prince Stasio calling off his wedding to Princess Beatriz."

"So it's already today's news in New York." He sounded far away. She watched him rub the back of his neck, something he did when he was pondering a grave problem.

Growing more uneasy, Dottie stood up. "Forgive me if I've upset you."

He eyed her frankly. "Forgiveness doesn't come into it. They were never suited, but I didn't know he'd made the break official until he told me last night."

She rubbed her arms in reaction. "What a traumatic night it must have been for all of you and your grandmother."

"I won't lie to you about that." His pain was palpable.

Dottie bit her lip. "For both their sakes I'm glad he couldn't go through with it, but you'll probably think I'm horrible for saying it."

"On the contrary," Alex ground out. "I'd think something serious was wrong with you if you hadn't. His life has been a living hell. He should have ended the betrothal years ago."

Alex... She heard the love for his brother.

"Does it mean the queen will go on ruling?" she

asked quietly. "I'm probably overstepping my bounds to talk to you like this, but after meeting your brother, I can't help but feel terrible for what he must be suffering right now, even if he didn't want the marriage."

"Between us, he's in bad shape," he confided, "but the coronation is still on. Our grandmother is failing in small ways and can't keep up her former pace as sovereign, but she's still in charge. She has given him six months to marry one of the eligible royals on her list."

"But—"

"There are no buts," he cut her off, but she knew his anger wasn't directed at her. "I just have to pray he'll find some common ground with one of the women." His voice throbbed. Again Dottie was horrified by Prince Stasio's untenable situation. "Since there's nothing I can do except stand by him, I'd rather concentrate on Zoe's lesson. What do you have planned for today?"

Heartsick as Dottie felt, she'd been sent to Hellenica to do a job and she wanted desperately to lift his spirits if she could. "Since we're on the yacht, I thought we'd work on the *Y* sound. She can already say *Yiayia* pretty well."

"That's where her Greek ought to help."

"Why don't you say hello to her in Greek and we'll see what happens."

Together they walked toward the railing at the far end. Zoe saw them coming and trained the binoculars on them.

"Yasoo," her father called to her. The cute little girl answered back in a sad facsimile of the greeting.

Dottie smiled. "Do you like being on this boat?"

"Yes."

Today they'd work on *ya*. Another day they'd work

on *yes*. "Do you know what kind of a boat this is?" Zoe shook her head. "It's called a yacht. Say *yasoo* again." Zoe responded. "Now say *ya*." She tried, but the sound was off with both words.

"I can't."

Dottie felt her frustration.

Alex handed Dottie the binoculars and picked up his daughter. "Try it once more." He wanted her to make a good sound for him. Dottie wanted it, too, more than anything. But this was a game of infinite patience. "Be a parrot for daddy, like one of those parrot fish you were watching with its birdlike beak. Parrots can talk. Talk to me. Say *ya*."

"Ya."

"Open your mouth wider like your daddy is doing," Dottie urged her. "Pretend he's the doctor looking down your throat with a stick. He wants to hear you. Can you say *ya* for him?"

She giggled. "Daddy's not a doctor."

The prince sent Dottie a look of defeat. "You're right." He kissed Zoe's cheek. "Come on. Let's have a lemonade." As soon as he put her down, she ran back to the table by the loungers to drink hers.

Clearly Zoe wasn't in the mood for a lesson. Who would be on a beautiful day like this? The translucent blue water was dotted with islands that made Dottie itch to get out and explore everything. She put the binoculars to her eyes to see what was coming next. "What's the name of that island in the distance?"

"Argentum."

"You mine silver there?"

"How did you figure that out?"

"You told me you lived on Aurum. Both islands have Latin names for gold and silver."

His eyes met hers. "You're not only intelligent, but knowledgeable. We'll anchor out in the bay. The head mining engineer is coming aboard for a business lunch. He's also my closest friend."

"Where did you meet?"

"We were getting our mining engineering degrees at the same time, both here and in Colorado at the school of mines."

"That's why your English is amazing. Is your friend married?"

"Yes. He has a new baby."

"That's nice for him."

"Very nice. He's in love with his wife and she with him."

Dottie couldn't bear to talk about that subject. "Tell me about the tall island beyond Argentum with the green patches?"

"That's Aurum, where Zoe and I normally live." He hadn't put on his shirt yet. She could feel his body radiating heat. "As you guessed correctly, rich gold deposits on the other side of the mountain were discovered there centuries ago. Bari and I are both passionate about our work. There are many more mining projects to be explored. I'm anxious to get back to them."

By now she was trembling from their close proximity. Needing a reason to move away from him, she put the binoculars on the table and picked up her lemonade. "Do you miss Aurum?"

"Yes." His dark gaze wandered over her, sending her pulse rate off the charts. "Zoe and I prefer it to Hellenica. The palace there is much smaller with more trees and vegetation that keep it cooler. We'll take you next week so Zoe can show you the garden off her room."

Dottie let the comment pass because if she were still here by then, she had no intention of going there with him. It wouldn't be a good idea. Not a good idea at all. "Do you get her to preschool by helicopter, then?"

He nodded. "Once she's in kindergarten, she'll go to a school on Aurum, but nothing is going to happen until after the coronation." After swallowing the contents of his drink without taking a breath, he reached for his shirt. "Shall we go below and freshen up before Bari comes on board?"

She followed the two of them down the steps of the elegant yacht to the luxurious cabins. "Come with us." Zoe pulled on her hand.

Dottie bent over. "I have my own cabin down the hallway."

"How come?"

"Because I'm a guest."

She looked at her daddy. "Make her come."

"Zoe? We have our room, and she has hers," he said in his princely parental voice as Dottie thought of it.

To the surprise of both of them, Zoe kept hold of Dottie's hand. "I want to be with you."

"It's all right, Your Highness," Dottie said before he could protest. "Zoe and I will freshen up together and meet you on deck in a little while." Their family was going through deep turmoil. The burden of what his brother had done had set off enormous ramifications and Alex was feeling them.

For that matter, so was Zoe, who'd behaved differently today. With the advent of Prince Stasio's stunning news, she couldn't have helped but pick up on the tension radiating from the queen and her father during breakfast. She might not understand all that was going on, but she sensed upheaval. That's why she'd given up on her lesson so easily.

His eyes narrowed in what she assumed was speculation. "You're sure?"

"Do you even have to ask?" Dottie had meant what she'd told him last week about his needing some pampering. He had work to do with Mr. Jouflas, but no one else was there to help him with Zoe the way he needed it. Dottie found she wanted to ease his burden. He'd made sacrifices for the love of his country. Now it was her turn, no matter how small.

"You're operating under an abnormal amount of strain right now. You could use a little help. I don't know how you've been doing this balancing act for such a long time." She smiled at Zoe. "Come on."

Dottie saw the relief on his face and knew she'd said the right thing. "In that case I'll send the steward to your cabin with a fresh change of clothes for her."

"That would be perfect."

CHAPTER SEVEN

DOTTIE felt Alex staring at her before they disappeared inside. Since she'd been trying so hard to keep a professional distance with his daughter, he knew this was an about-face for her. But no one could have foreseen this monarchial disaster.

Alex was being torn apart by his love for his brother, his grandmother and the future of the crown itself. He was Atlas holding up the world with no help in sight. This was a day like no other. If Dottie could ease a little of his burden where Zoe was concerned, then she wanted to.

"I've got an idea, Zoe. After you shower, we'll take a little nap on the beds. The heat has made me sleepy."

"Me, too."

There were two queen beds. Before long she'd tucked Zoe under the covers.

"Dot? Will you please stay with Daddy and me forever? I know you're not my mommy, but Daddy said you were once a mommy."

She struggled for breath. "Yes. I had a little boy named Cory who had to work on his speech, just like you."

"What happened to him?"

"He died in a car accident with my husband."

"So you're all alone."

"Yes," she murmured, but for the first time it wasn't hard to talk about. The conversation with Alex last night had been cathartic.

"My mommy died and now Daddy and I are all alone."

"Except that you have your great-grandmother and your uncle."

"But I want you."

Dottie wanted to be with Zoe all the time, too. Somehow she'd gotten beyond her deep sadness and would love to care permanently for this child. But it was impossible in too many ways to even consider.

"Let's be happy we're together right now, shall we?" she said in a shaky voice.

"Yes." Zoe finally closed her eyes and fell asleep.

Dotti took her own shower and dressed in a clean pair of jeans and a blouse. When she came out of the bathroom, the other bed looked inviting. She thought she'd lie down on top while she waited for Zoe to wake up.

The next thing she knew, she heard a familiar male voice whispering her name. Slightly disoriented, she rolled over and discovered Alex sitting on the side of the bed. She'd been dreaming about him, but to see his gorgeous self in the flesh this close to her gave her heart a serious workout. His eyes were like black fires. They trapped hers, making it impossible for her to look away.

"Thank you for stepping in."

She studied his features. "I wanted to."

"With your help I was able to conclude our business lunch in record time and came in to bring Zoe a change of clothes. Do you have any idea how beautiful you are lying there?"

Dottie couldn't swallow. She tried to move away, but he put an arm across her body so she was tethered to him. "Please let me go," she begged. "Zoe will be awake any minute now."

He leaned over her, running a hand up her arm. The feel of skin against hot skin brought every nerve ending alive. "I'll take any minute I can steal. Being alone with you is all I've been able to think about."

"Alex—" she cried as his dark head descended.

"I love it when you say my name in that husky voice." He covered her mouth with his own in an exploratory kiss as if this were their first time and they were in no hurry whatsoever. He took things slow in the beginning, tantalizing her until it wasn't enough. Then their kiss grew deeper and more sensuous. His restless lips traveled over every centimeter of her face and throat before capturing her mouth again and again.

The other night he'd kindled a fire in her that had never died down. Now his mastery conjured the flames licking through her body with the speed of a forest fire in full conflagration.

Out of breath, he buried his face in the side of her neck. "I want you, Dottie. I've never wanted any woman so much, and I know you want me."

"I think that's been established," she admitted against his jaw that hadn't seen a razor since early morning. She delighted in every masculine line and angle of his well-honed body. With legs and arms entwined, their mouths clung as their passion grew more frenzied. They tried to appease their hunger, but no kiss was long enough or deep enough to satisfy the desire building.

He'd taken them to a new level. She felt cherished. Like the wedding vow repeated by the groom, it seemed as if Alex was worshipping her with his body. But in the midst of this rapture only he could have created, she heard the blare of a ship's horn. With it came the realization that this was no wedding night and a groan escaped her throat.

She'd actually been making out with Prince Alexius of Hellenica on his royal yacht! Never mind that it was the middle of the day and his daughter was asleep in the next bed. What if Zoe had awakened and had been watching them?

Horrified to have gotten this carried away, Dottie wrenched her mouth from his and slipped out of his arms. So deep was his entrancement, she'd caught him off guard. Thankfully she was able to get to her feet before he could prevent it, but in her weakened state she almost fell over.

"Dottie?" he called her name in longing, but she didn't dare stay in here and be seduced by the spell he'd cast over her. On the way out of the cabin she grabbed her purse and hurried down the corridor to the stairs.

At the top of the gangway the deck steward smiled at her. "Mrs. Richards? We've docked on Hellenica. You're welcome to go ashore whenever you please."

Could he tell she'd been kissed breathless by the prince? The sun she'd picked up couldn't account for mussed hair and swollen lips, too.

The queen didn't deserve to hear this bit of gossip on top of Prince Stasio's shocking news. Every second Dottie stayed on board, she was contributing to more court intrigue. She couldn't bear it. In fact she couldn't believe they were back at the main island already. She'd been in such a completely different world with Alex, she'd lost track of everything including her wits.

"Th-thank you," her voice faltered. Without hesitation, she left the yacht and got in the waiting limousine. While she was still alone, she brushed her hair and applied some lipstick, trying to make herself presentable.

A few minutes later Alex approached the car with Zoe. "Dot!" she cried and climbed in next to her.

"Did you just wake up?" Dottie concentrated on Zoe, studiously avoiding his eyes. "You were a sleepyhead."

Zoe thought that was funny. She chatted happily with her daddy until they reached the palace where Hector stood outside the entry.

"Welcome back, Your Highness. The queen is waiting for you and the princess to join her and Prince Stasio in her suite."

A royal summons. It didn't surprise Dottie. She'd had visions of the queen herself waiting for them as they drove up to the entrance. For an instant she caught Alex's enigmatic glance before he alighted from the car. All their lives he and Stasio had been forced to obey that summons. A lesser person would have broken long before now.

She might be an outsider, yet she couldn't help but want to rebel against this antiquated system she'd only read about in history books. Unbelievable that it was still going on in the twenty-first century!

Alex helped them out of the backseat. "Come on, Dot." Zoe's hand had slipped into hers. She had to harden herself against Zoe's plea. The child's emotional hold on her was growing stronger with every passing day.

"I'm sorry. The queen has asked for you and your

daddy to come, and I have to speak to my director in New York." Aware Alex's eyes were on her she said, "You have to go with him. I'll see you tomorrow when we leave for your preschool."

Gripping the bag tighter, Dottie hurried inside the palace doors and raced up the stairs. She fled to her suite pursued by demons she'd been fighting from the beginning. Since this afternoon when she'd fallen into Alex's arms like a ripe plum, those demons had gained a foothold, making her situation precarious.

Her instincts told her to pack her bags and fly back to New York tonight. But if she were to just up and leave Hellenica, it would only exacerbate an already volatile situation with Zoe, who'd poured her heart out to her earlier.

Without hesitation she marched over to the bed and reached for the house phone. "This is Mrs. Richards. Could you bring a car around for me? I'm going into the city." She'd eat dinner somewhere and do some more sightseeing. After the nap she'd had, it might take hours before she was ready for bed again.

Alex waited for Hector to alert him on the phone. When the call came, he learned Dottie had just returned to the palace. He checked his watch. Ten to ten.

He left Zoe's bedroom and waited for Dottie at the top of the stairs leading to her suite. This time he didn't step out of the shadows. He stood there in full view. Halfway up she caught sight of him and slowed her steps. Alarm was written all over her beautiful face. She'd picked up some sun earlier in the day, adding appealing color.

"Alex? What's wrong?"

Anyone watching them would never know what had gone on between them on the yacht. He'd nearly made love to her and her passion had equalled his. Her breathtaking response had changed his life today.

"Let's just say there's a lot wrong around here. Since your arrival in Hellenica, you've got me skulking in every conceivable place in order to find time alone with you. At this point you'd have reason to think I'm your personal phantom of the opera." He drew in a harsh breath. "We have to talk, but not here." When he saw her stiffen he said, "I know you can't be commanded, but I'm asking you to come with me as a personal favor." He'd constructed his words carefully.

Tension sizzled between them as he started down the stairs toward her. To his relief she didn't fight him. Slowly she followed him to the main floor. They went down the hallway and out a side door where he'd asked that his sports car be brought around.

Alex saw the question in her eyes. "I bought this ten years ago. It's my getaway car when I need to be alone to think." He intentionally let her get in by herself because he didn't trust himself not to touch her. After leaving the grounds, he headed for the road leading to an isolated portion of the coast with rocky terrain.

"But you're *not* alone," she said in a haunted whisper.

"If you mean the bodyguards, you're right." He felt her nervousness. "Relax. If I had seduction in mind, we wouldn't be in this. I purposely chose it in order to keep my hands off you tonight."

"Alex—"

"Let me finish," he interrupted. "Whatever you may think about me, I'm not in the habit of luring available women to my bed when the mood strikes me. You came to Hellenica at my request in order to test Zoe. Neither of us could have predicted what would happen after you arrived.

"I can't speak for you, but I know for a fact that even if your husband's memory will always be in your heart, the chemistry between us is more powerful than anything I've ever felt in my life. We both know it's not going to go away."

She lowered her head.

"One night with you could never be enough for me." He gripped the steering wheel tighter. "I know you would never consent to be my mistress, and I would never ask you. But until the coronation is over, I'm requesting your help with Zoe."

She shifted in the seat. "In what way?"

"Stasio and my daughter both need me desperately, but I can't be in two places at the same time and still manage the daily affairs of the crown. My brother is going through the blackest period of his life. He's clinging to me and shutting out our grandmother. She's beside herself."

"I can only imagine."

"I'm worried about both of them and asked the doctor to come. He's with them now, seeing what can be done to get them through this nightmare. He says I need to be there for Stasio 24/7. I've asked our cousin Philippe to fly here and stay for a few days so my brother has someone to talk to he trusts."

"I'm so sorry, Alex."

"So am I," he muttered morosely. "This situation is something that's been coming on for years. Unfortunately it's had a negative impact on Zoe. When we got back to the palace today, it took me an hour to settle her down. She wanted to go to your room with you. Tonight she begged me to let you become her official nanny."

Alex heard a half-smothered moan come out of Dottie. The sound tore him up because any kind of connection to keep her with him was fading fast. "It wouldn't work."

"You think I don't know that?" he bit out. "But as a temporary solution, would you be willing to stay at the palace on Aurum with her until the coronation? She loves it there, especially the garden. One of the staff has grandchildren she plays with. I'd fly over each evening in the helicopter to say good-night.

"When the coronation is over, I'll be moving back to Aurum with Zoe, and you can return to New York. Hector will see to your flight arrangements. I assume your replacement will arrive soon after that, if not before. But until then, can I rely on your help?"

She nodded without looking at him. "Of course."

The bands constricting his breathing loosened a little. "Thank you. On Saturday I'll run you and Zoe over in the cruiser. We'll skip her preschool next week."

"Are you still going to go ahead with the arrangements for the Varney boy to come home with Zoe after class tomorrow?"

"Yes," he murmured. "Any distraction would be better than her being around my grandmother, who's not in a good way right now. She's always been a rock, but she never saw this coming with Stasio."

"You sound exhausted, Alex. Tomorrow will be here before we know it. Let's go back to the palace."

She sounded like Hector. *Go back. Do your duty. Forget you're a man with a man's needs.*

Full of rage, he made a sharp U-turn and sped toward the palace tight-lipped, but by the time they reached the entry, he'd turned into one aching entity of pain. He watched the only person who could take it away for good rush away on her gorgeous legs.

Dottie could tell Zoe felt shy around Mark Varney. She stuck close to her daddy at the shallow end of the pool.

They'd just returned home from the preschool. Mark was a cute, dark blond first grader who sported a marine haircut and was a good little swimmer already. He didn't appear to be nervous as he floated on an inner tube at the deep end, kicking his strong legs. Dottie sat on the edge by him.

"My mom told me she talks funny. How come?" he said quietly.

"Sometimes a child can't make sounds come out the way they want. But I'm working on them with her. One day she'll sound like you, but for now I'm hoping to get your help."

He blinked. "How? She's a princess."

She looked at his boyish face with its smattering of freckles. "Forget about that. She's a girl. Just be friends with her. In a way, you can be her best teacher."

His sunny blue eyes widened. "I can?"

"Yes. You're older and you're an American who speaks English very well. If you'll play with her, she'll listen to you when you talk and she'll try to sound like you. You're a guy, and guys like to dare each other, right?"

He grinned. "Yeah."

"Well, start daring her. You know. Tell her you bet she can't say *bat*."

"Bat?" He laughed.

"She's working on her *B*'s and *T*'s. Make a game out of it. Tell her that if she can say *bat* right, you'll show her your MP3 player. I saw you playing with it in the limo on the drive to the palace."

"Don't tell my dad. I'm not supposed to take it to school."

She studied him for a minute. "If he finds out, I'll tell him you're using it to help Zoe. She's never seen one of those. There's an application on it that makes those animal sounds."

"Oh, yeah—"

"It'll fascinate her."

"Cool."

"See if you can get her to say *cool*, too."

"Okay. This is fun."

Dottie was glad he thought so. After trying to learn Greek at school and home, it had to be a big release for him to speak English. "Let's go have a war with her and her daddy." She took off her beach coat and slipped into the water. "You get on the whale. I'll push you over to them and we'll start splashing."

"Won't the prince get mad?"

"Yes." Dottie smiled. "Real mad."

His face lit up and they took off.

Hopefully Alex would get mad enough to forget his own problems for a little while. She'd suffered for him and his family all night. No matter her misgivings about spending full days with Zoe until the coronation, she couldn't have turned Alex down last night. The look in his expression had been a study in anguish, aging him.

Once they reached their destination, the happy shrieks coming out of Zoe were just the thing to get their war started. For a good ten minutes they battled as if their lives depended on it. The best sound of all was Alex's full-bodied laughter. After knowing how deeply he'd been affected by his family's problems, Dottie hadn't expected to hear it again.

When she came up for air after Alex's last powerful dunk, his eyes were leveled on her features. "You've been holding out on me. All this time I thought maybe you couldn't swim well. I was going to offer to teach you, but I was afraid you'd think I was a lecherous old man wanting to get my hands on you. After I showed up in your cabin on the yacht, now you know it's true."

She was thankful for the water that cooled her instantly hot cheeks. In the periphery she noticed Mark pushing Zoe around on the whale. He was talking a blue streak and had captured her full attention. The ice had been broken and they were oblivious to everyone else. Dottie couldn't have been more pleased.

Alex followed her gaze. "Your experiment is working. She's so excited by his attention, she hasn't once called for either of us."

"I've asked him to help her. He's a darling boy." In the next few minutes she told Alex about their conversation. "If all goes well today, how would you feel about Mark coming home with us from school on Friday?"

"I'm open to anything that will help her speech improve and make her happy."

"Mark seems to be doing both. I've learned he's been unhappy, so I was thinking maybe he could even come to Aurum with us on Saturday. Naturally you'd have to talk to his parents. If they're willing, maybe he could make a visit to the island next week. You know, after his morning class at preschool. Zoe would have something exciting to look forward to and I know it would be good for him, too."

His eyes glinted with an emotion she couldn't read. "I can see where you're going with this. If you think his being there will prevent her attachment to you from growing deeper, you couldn't be more wrong. But as a plan to entertain them and help her, I like the idea."

"Honestly?"

He ran suntanned hands through his wet black hair. Adonis couldn't possibly have been as attractive. "I wouldn't have said so otherwise."

She expelled the breath she'd been holding. "Thank you. I was thinking Zoe and I could ride the ferry to Hellenica and meet him at the dock after he's out of class. He could ride back with us and we could eat lunch on board. Mark can help her pronounce the names of foods, and she can teach him some more Greek words."

Alex nodded. "I'll fly him back with me in the helicopter in the evening."

"You'd be willing to do that?"

He frowned. "By now I thought it was clear to you I'd do anything to help my daughter. In order to ensure that you stay with her until her uncle Stasi has been proclaimed king, I've even gone so far as to promise I won't touch you again."

She knew that and already felt the cost of it.

If he had any comprehension of how hard this was for her, too... They had no future together, but that didn't mean she found it easy to keep her distance. She'd come alive in his arms. Because she was unable to assuage these yearnings, the pleasure had turned on her so she was in continual pain. This was the precise reason she didn't want to have feelings for any man, not ever again, but it was far too late for that.

"Your Highness?"

Hector's voice intruded, producing a grimace from Alex. Dottie hadn't realized he'd come out to the pool. It seemed like every time she found herself in a private conversation with Alex, some force was afoot that kept wedging them further apart, At this point she was a mass of contradictions. Her head told her the interruption was for the best, but her heart—oh, her heart. It hammered mercilessly.

"King Alexandre-Philippe has arrived from Valleder and your presence is requested in the queen's drawing room. The ministers have been assembled."

Hearing that news, Alex's face became an inscrutable mask. "Thank you, Hector. Tell her I'll be there shortly."

His gaze shot to Dottie's. "I'm afraid this will be a long night. I'd better slip away now while Zoe's having fun."

"I think that's a good idea. We'll walk Mark out to his parents' car before dinner. She can eat with me. Later I'll take her to her bedroom and put her down."

"You couldn't have any comprehension of what it means to me to know you're taking care of my daughter. Sofia will be there to help. I'll try to get away long enough to kiss her good-night, but I can't promise."

"I understand."

"If I don't make it, I'll see you at nine in the morning. After I've talked to Mark's parents, we'll see if he wants to join us on Saturday. I thought we'd take the cruiser to Aurum. Sofia will know what to pack for Zoe."

"We'll be ready."

She heard his sharp intake of breath. "Zoe trusts you and loves being with you. Under the circumstances, it's an enormous relief to me."

"I'm glad. As for me, she's a joy to be with, Your Highness." She had to keep calling him by his title to remind herself of the great gulf between them no ordinary human could bridge. If she were a princess...

But she wasn't! And if she'd been born a royal, he would have run in the other direction.

For him, any attraction to her stemmed from forbidden fruit. She was a commoner. It was the nature of a man or woman to desire what they couldn't or shouldn't have. In that regard they were both cursed!

Fathoms deep in turmoil, she noticed his eyes lingering on the curve of her mouth for a moment. She glimpsed banked fires in those incredibly dark recesses. He was remembering those moments on the yacht, too. Dottie could feel it and the look he was giving her ignited her senses to a feverish pitch.

With effortless male agility he suddenly levered himself from the pool and disappeared inside the palace. When he was gone, the loss she felt was staggering.

CHAPTER EIGHT

"HI, MARK!"

"Hi!"

He got out of his father's limo and hurried along the dock to get in the cruiser. Zoe's brown eyes lit up when she saw him. The two fathers spoke for a minute longer before Alex joined them and made sure everyone put on a life preserver.

The prince piloted the boat himself and they took off. Excitement suffused Dottie, crowding out any misgivings for the moment. She found the day was too wonderful. It seemed the children did, too. Both wore a perpetual smile on their animated faces. Zoe pointed out more fish and birds as they drew closer to their destination. While they were communicating, Alex darted Dottie an amused glance.

She wondered if he was thinking what she'd been thinking. What if his daughter and Mark were to share a friendship that took them through childhood to the teenage years? What if... But she forced her mind to turn off and think only happy thoughts. The island of Aurum was coming up fast. She'd concentrate on it.

Somehow she'd assumed it shared many of the characteristics of Hellenica, but the mountains were higher and woodier. As they pulled up to the royal dock, Dottie had to admit her adrenaline had been surging in anticipation of seeing where they lived. When Alex talked about Aurum, she noticed his voice dropped to a deeper level because he loved it here.

He'd explained that the mountainous part of the island where the palace was located had been walled off from the public. This had been his private residence from the age of eighteen and would continue to be for as long as he retained the title of Duke of Aurum. She'd learned it had its own game preserve, a wildlife sanctuary, a bird refuge and a stable.

Somehow she'd expected this palace to resemble the white Cycladic style of that on Hellenica. Nothing could have been further from the truth. Through the heavy foliage she glimpsed a small gem of Moorish architecture in the form of a square, all on one level.

"Oh!" she cried out in instant delight the second she saw it from the open limo window.

Alex heard her. "This area of the Aegean has known many civilizations. If you'll notice, the other palace leaves the stairs and patios open. Everything tumbles to the sea. You'll see the reverse is true here. The Moors liked their treasures hidden within the walls."

"Whoa!" Mark exclaimed. His eyes widened in amazement. He'd stopped talking to Zoe. *Whoa* was the perfect word, all right.

Dottie marveled over the exterior, a weathered yellow and pale orange combination of seamless blocks delineated by stylized horizontal stripes, exquisite in detail. The limo passed a woman who looked about fifty standing at the arched entry into a courtyard laid out in ancient tiles surrounding a pool and an exquisite garden. At its center stood a latticed gazebo. This was the garden Alex had referred to last week.

As he helped them from the car, a peacock peered from behind some fronds and unexpectedly opened its plumage. The whirring sound startled Dottie and Mark, but Zoe only laughed. It walked slowly, displaying its glorious fan.

"Whoa," their guest said again, incredulous over what he was seeing. It *was* hard to believe.

Dottie eyed Alex. "We're definitely going to have to work on the *P* sound."

One corner of his mouth curved upward. He ran a hand over his chest covered by a cream-colored polo shirt. "Don't look now," he said quietly, "but there's a partridge in the peach tree behind you."

Slowly she turned around, thinking he was teasing her while he made the *P* sounds. But he'd told the truth!

Transfixed, she shook her head, examining everything in sight. A profusion of pink and orange flowers grew against the gazebo. She walked through the scrolling pathway toward it. Inside she discovered a lacy looking set of chairs and a table inlaid with mother-of-pearl. Dottie felt as if she'd just walked inside the pages of a rare first-edition history book of the Ottoman empire. This couldn't possibly be real.

Alex must have understood what she was feeling because he flashed her a white smile. But this one was different because it was carefree. For a brief moment she'd been given a glimpse of what he might have looked like years ago, before he'd had a true understanding that he was Prince Alexius Constantinides with obligations and serious responsibilities he would have to shoulder for the rest of his life.

There was a sweetness in his expression, the same sweetness she saw in Zoe when she was really happy about something, like right now. But the moment was bittersweet for Dottie when she thought of the pain waiting for him back on Hellenica. A myriad of emotions tightened her chest because her pain was mixed up in there, too.

"Do you want to see my room?" Zoe asked Mark.

"I want to follow the peacock first."

"Okay." She tagged along with her new friend, still managing to carry Baby Betty in her hands.

Alex spread his strong arms. "Guys and girls. Human nature doesn't change." Dottie laughed gently, sharing this electric moment with him.

Porticos with bougainvillea and passion flowers joined one section of the palace to the other. The alcoved rooms were hidden behind. Zoe's was a dream of Moorish tiles and unique pieces of furniture with gold leaf carved years ago by a master palace craftsman of that earlier civilization.

A silky, pale pink fabric formed the canopy and covering of her bed. Near a tall hutch filled with her treasures stood an exquisite pink rose tree. When Dottie looked all the way up, she gasped at the sheer beauty of the carved ceiling with hand-painted roses and birds.

Alex had been watching her reaction. "Your room is next door. Would you like to see it?"

Speechless, she nodded and followed him through an alcove to another masterpiece of design similar to Zoe's except for the color scheme. "Whoever painted the cornflowers in this room must have had your eyes in mind, Dottie. They grow wild on the hillsides. You'll see them when you and Zoe go hiking or horseback riding."

She was spellbound. Her eyes fell to the bed canopied with blue silk. "Was this the room you and your wife used? It's breathtaking."

In a flash his facial muscles tensed up. "Teresa never lived here with me. Like my grandmother, she preferred the palace on Hellenica. She thought this place too exotic and isolated, the mountains too savage. This room was used during my mother's time for guests. Since Teresa's death, Zoe's string of nannies have lived in here."

Dottie couldn't help but speculate on how much time he and his wife must have spent apart—that is, when they didn't have to perform certain civic duties together. Separation went on in unhappy marriages all over the planet, but this was different. He'd been born into a family where duty dictated his choice of bride. Even cocooned in this kind of luxury only a few people would ever know, the onlooker could expect such an arrangement to fail.

As Dottie's aunt had often told her, "You're a romantic, Dottie. For that reason you can be hurt the worst. Why set yourself up, honey?" Good question. Dottie's heart ached for Alex and Stasio, for Teresa and Beatriz, for Genevieve, for every royal who had a role and couldn't deviate from it.

"My apartment is through the next alcove. The last section houses two more guest rooms plus the kitchen and dining room. There's a den where I do my work. It has television and a computer. All of it is at your disposal for the time you're here."

"I've never seen anything so unusual and beautiful."

"Those are my sentiments, too. You saw Inez when we drove in. She and her husband, Ari, head the staff here. There's the gamekeeper, of course, and Thomas who runs the stable. All you have to do is pick up the phone and Inez will direct one of the maids to help you."

"Thank you. I didn't expect to find paradise when I came to Hellenica. I don't think your brother believed me when I told him it really does exists here."

"Paradise implies marital bliss. You'll have to forgive him for being cynical over your naïveté."

Alex's comment bordered on mockery, revealing emotions too raw for him to hide. She shuddered and turned away, not wanting to see the bleakness she often saw in his eyes when he didn't know she was looking.

"I'd better go check on Zoe." She hurried through to the other bedroom, but there was still no sign of her.

Alex came up behind Dottie, close enough for her to feel the warmth of his breath on her neck. "I'll give you one guess where she's gone."

"Well, Mark is pretty cute. She doesn't know she's playing with fire yet." The words came out too fast for her to stop them.

"That's true," Alex said in a gravelly voice before she was spun around and crushed against him. "But I do, and right now I don't give a damn. I want you so badly I'm shaking." He put her hand on his chest. "Feel that thundering? It's my heart. That's what you do to me. I know I promised not to touch you, but I'm not strong enough to keep it. You're going to have to give me help."

The moment had caught her unaware. He had a slumberous look in his eyes. His mouth was too close. She couldn't think, couldn't breathe. Dottie tried to remove her hand, but found her limbs had grown weak with longings that had taken over.

"Alex—" She half groaned his name before taking the initiative to kiss him. When she realized she'd been the one to make it happen, it was too late to change her mind. Their mouths met in mutual hunger. She wrapped her arms around his neck, wanting to merge with him.

With one hand cupping the back of her head, his other wandered over her spine and hips, drawing her closer. The kiss she'd started went on and on. She desired him too terribly to do anything that would cut off the divine experience of giving and taking pleasure like this.

In the background she heard the children's muffled laughter. She didn't know if they'd peeked in this room and had seen them or not, but the sound was too close for comfort. Much as she never wanted to leave Alex's arms, she slid her hands back down his chest and tried to ease away from him so he would relinquish her mouth.

"I heard them," he whispered before she could say anything. Alex had the uncanny ability to read her mind.

"I hope Zoe didn't see us."

He sucked in his breath and cupped her face in his hands. "I hate to break this to you, but she woke at the last minute on the yacht."

Guilt swept through her, making her whole body go white-hot.

"Every little four-year-old girl has seen the movie of *Snow White*. My Zoe knows that when Prince Charming kissed the princess awake, it was true love that worked the charm."

What he was telling her now caused Dottie's body to shake with fright. "You don't think she really sees us that way—"

His handsome features hardened. "Who's to say? In her eyes you're her mommy. Zoe has never seen me kiss another woman. I *have* brought you to my castle. The way you and I were devouring each other just now has probably set the seal in her mind."

Aghast, Dottie propelled herself away from him. "Then you have to unset it, Alex."

"I'm afraid it's too late. You might as well know the rest."

She folded her arms to her waist to stay calm. "What more is there?"

"Sofia had a private word with me this morning before I left the palace. Just as Hector spies for my grandmother, Sofia is my eyes and ears where Zoe is concerned. It seems my daughter told her grandmother that you and I were leaving for Aurum today. But she told her not to cry. When we have the baby, we'll bring it to see *Yiayia*."

Dottie didn't know whether to laugh or cry, but the tears won out. The sound that escaped her lips was probably as unintelligible as Zoe's word for Hector. Four consonants. All difficult. "Your grandmother's world truly has come crashing down on her."

She saw his body tauten before he caught her in his arms once more. He shook her gently. "What has happened between you and me wasn't planned. For two years I've been telling the queen I'll never marry again, so it's absurd for you to be feeling guilt of any kind over Genevieve." He kissed her wet eyelids, then her whole face.

"It's not so much guilt as the *fear* I feel for Zoe. She's attached herself to me because of her speech problem. I won't be here much longer, but every day that I stay, it's going to make the ultimate separation that much harder."

A shudder passed through his body she could feel. "You think I'm not aware of that?"

She broke free of him. "I know you are, but we've got to lay down some ground rules. I don't ever want her to see us together like we are now. We can't be alone again. This has to be the end so she won't fantasize about us, Alex. It's no good. I'm going to my room to unpack and settle in. Go be with her and Mark right now. Please."

Blind with pain, she left him standing there ashen-faced.

On Wednesday evening of the following week, Alex's mood was as foul as Stasio's. Five days ago Dottie had virtually told him goodbye on the island, but he couldn't handle it any longer and needed to see her. Something had to be done or he was going to go out of his mind.

Philippe had just left to fly home to Vallader, but he would be coming back with his family to attend the coronation on Saturday just a week off now. Until then Alex and his brother were alone.

Stasio cast him a probing glance. "I do believe you're as restless as I am."

Alex gritted his teeth. "You're right." He shot to his feet. "Alert security and come with me. I'm leaving for Aurum to say good-night to Zoe."

"*And* Dottie?"

"I don't want to talk about her. After Zoe's asleep we'll do some riding and camp out in the mountains."

At least that was what he was telling himself now. Wild with pain, he spun around.

"When it comes to a woman, I can't have what I really want. Even if I could, she wouldn't want me. She adored her husband. Why do you think she's still single? No man measures up. The day after your coronation, she'll be leaving the country whether the new speech therapist replacing her has arrived or not."

"Zoe won't stand for it."

"She'll *have* to," he said in a hoarse whisper. "We're all going to have to go on doing our duty. You've never been able to have what you really wanted. You think I don't know what's been going on inside of you? It's killing me."

Stasio stopped midstride. His tormented expression said it all. "What do you want to do, little brother?"

Alex's brows had formed a black bar above his eyes. "Let's get out of here. Gather anything you need and I'll meet you at the helipad."

Before long they were winging their way to Aurum. Once they'd landed, Zoe came running with a couple of the other children who lived on the estate. Inez chatted with him for a minute.

Alex picked up his daughter and hugged her hard. "I've missed you."

"I've been waiting for you, Daddy. I missed you, too."

He kissed her curls. "Where's Dottie?"

"In town." Tears crept down her cheeks. "She said I couldn't go with her."

Naturally Zoe hadn't been happy about that. Though Alex couldn't argue with Dottie's decision, the news sent his heart plunging to his feet. She'd warned him that she would never be alone with him again and she'd meant it.

"How about a hug for me!" Stasio drew her into his arms to give Alex a chance to pull himself together.

Inez gathered up the other children, leaving the men alone with Zoe. They talked about Mark. "I'm sorry he had a cold and couldn't come today."

"Do you think he can come tomorrow?"

"I'll find out."

"I know he wants to come. Dot told us that after our lesson she'd take us out to look for ducks. He can't wait!"

Of course he couldn't. Any time spent with Dottie was pure enchantment.

"Will you ask his mommy?"

"You know I will."

Stasio put a hand on his shoulder. "I'll be at the stable getting the horses ready."

He nodded. "Come on, my little princess. It's getting late. Time to go to bed."

As she chatted with him, he realized he was starting to hear true sounds coming out of her and she was doing a lot more talking. In a month's time Dottie had already made a profound difference in her. All the thanks in the world would never be able to express his gratitude adequately to her.

For the next half hour he read stories to Zoe, then it was time for her prayers. At the end she said, "Bless my daddy and my Dot."

He blinked. She'd said *Dot* distinctly! He'd heard the *D* and the *T*, plus the *ah* in the middle.

Tears sprang to his eyes. This was Dottie's doing. She'd been trying to get her to say *Dot* instead of *mommy*. Just now the word had passed Zoe's lips naturally. A miracle had happened. He wanted to shout his elation, but he didn't dare because she was ready to go to sleep.

The sudden realization hit Alex hard. He loved Dottie Richards. He loved her to the depth of his being. He wanted her in his life forever and needed to tell her so she wouldn't leave him or Zoe. There had to be a way to keep her here and he was going to find it.

Once his daughter was dead to the world, he stole out of her room and raced to the stable to tell his brother there'd been a major breakthrough with Zoe. It was providential he and Stasio were going riding. Alex did his best thinking on the back of a horse. Tonight he would need all his powers of reasoning to come up with a solution.

But as he approached his brother, Stasio's phone rang. One look at his face after he'd picked up and Alex knew there was trouble.

"That was Hector," he said after ringing off. "*Yiayia* isn't well. The doctor is with her, but he thinks we should come home." They stared at each other. With the queen ill, their best-laid plans would have to wait.

Alex informed Inez. By tacit agreement they left for the helipad. Tonight's shining moment with Zoe had been swallowed up in this new crisis with their grandmother. When they arrived back on Hellenica, Hector was waiting for them in their grandmother's suite.

"The doctor has already left. He says the queen's ulcer is acting up again. He gave her medicine for it and now she's sleeping comfortably. I'm sorry to have bothered you."

Stasio eyed Alex in relief. "Thanks for letting us

know, Hector. It could have been much more serious. We're glad you told us."

"Thank you for your understanding, Your Highness."

"You've been with our grandmother much longer than we have. No one's been more devoted." Stasio's glance rested on Alex. "Shall we go to my suite?"

He nodded at his brother. Both of them needed a good stiff drink about now. As he turned to leave, Hector cleared his throat. "Prince Alexius? If I may have a private word with you first."

Something strange was going on for Hector to address him so formally. Alex eyed his brother who looked equally baffled. "I'll be with you in a minute, Stasi."

After he walked off, Hector said, "Could we talk in your suite, Your Highness?"

"Of course." But the request was unprecedented. As they headed to his apartment, Alex had an unpleasant foreboding. Their grandmother was probably sicker than Hector had let on, but he didn't want to burden Stasio, who walked around with enough guilt for a defeated army. The decision to call off his wedding to Beatriz had dealt a near-lethal blow to their grandmother, and poor Hector had been caught in the fallout.

Once they'd entered the living room, Alex invited the older man to sit down, but he insisted on remaining standing, so they faced each other.

"You have my complete attention, Hector. What is it?"

"When's my daddy coming?"

Dottie had been swimming in the pool on Aurum with Zoe while they waited for Alex. "Last night he told you he would be here after your lesson, didn't he?"

"Yes. I want him to hurry. I hope Mark's still not sick."

"We'll find out soon enough, because I can hear your daddy's helicopter." They both looked up.

When Dottie saw it, the realization that Alex would be walking out here in a few minutes almost put her into cardiac arrest. No mere hormones or physical attraction to a man could cause these feelings that made her world light up just to hear his name or know he was in the vicinity.

She was in love. She knew that now. She was in love again, for the second time in her life, and she cried out at the injustice. Her first love and son had been struck down so cruelly, she'd wondered how she could ever build another life for herself.

Now here she was carrying on with her career and doomed to love again, only this man was a prince who was off-limits to her. By the time of the coronation, Zoe would be snatched from her, too, and she'd be left a totally empty vessel. Blackness weighed her down. *What am I going to do?*

While Zoe shouted with excitement and hurried across the tiles to meet her father, who'd be striding through the entry any second, Dottie got out of the pool and raced to her own room. To be with him would only succeed in pouring acid on a newly opened wound that would never heal.

Knowing Alex needed time alone with his daughter, Dottie would give it to him. Quickly she showered and changed into denims and a top before checking her emails. Dr. Rice had sent her another message.

Dear Mrs. Richards,
Success at last. Your replacement's name is Mrs.
Miriam Hawes. She'll be arriving in Athens to-
morrow. All the arrangements have been made.
When you return to New York, I have a new three-
year-old girl who needs testing. We'll enjoy hav-
ing you back. Good luck and keep me posted.
Dr. Rice.

Dottie read the words again before burying her face in her hands. While she was sobbing, a little princess came running into her room and caught her in the act.

"Why are you crying?" She put her face right up against Dottie's. "Do you have a boo-boo?"

Zoe could say boo-boo well enough to be understood. Nothing could have pleased Dottie more, but right now pain consumed her. Yes. Dottie had a big boo-boo, one that had crumbled her heart into tiny pieces.

She sniffed and wiped the moisture off her face. "I hurt myself getting out of the pool." It wasn't a lie. In her haste she'd scraped her thigh on the side, but she would live. "Did Mark come?"

"Yes. He's running after the peacock." Dottie laughed through the tears. "Can he pull out one of its big feathers?"

"No, darling. That would hurt it."

"Oh." Obviously she hadn't thought about that aspect. "Daddy wants you to come."

Dottie had wondered when the bell would toll. She had no choice but to walk out and say hello to Alex and Mark, who were already in the pool whooping it up. Zoe ran to join them.

"Good afternoon, Your Highness."

His all-encompassing black gaze swept over her. "Good afternoon," he said in his deep, sensuous voice. Her body quickened at the change in him from last Saturday when there'd been nothing but painful tension between them.

"I'm glad you brought Mark with you. How are you feeling today, Mark?"

"Good. I didn't have a temperature, so my mom said I could come."

Dottie took her usual place on the edge and dangled her bare feet in the water. "Well we're very happy you're here, aren't we, Zoe?" She nodded while she hung on to her daddy's neck. "Zoe tells me you'd like to take a peacock feather home for a souvenir."

"Yeah. Could I?"

The sudden glance Alex flashed Dottie was filled with mirth. He wasn't the same man of a few days ago. She hardly recognized him. "What do you say about that, Prince Alexius?"

By now he'd put Zoe up on his powerful shoulders. He looked like a god come to life. "Tell you what, Mark. That peacock is going to moult in another month. When he does, he'll shed his tail feathers. You and Zoe can follow him around. When he drops them, you can take home as many as he leaves."

"Thanks!"

"Cool, Daddy."

Alex burst into laughter. "What did you just say to me?"

"'Cool,'" Mark answered for her.

"That's what I thought she said."

"I've been teaching her."

Zoe patted her daddy's head. "Can Mark come to Uncle Stasi's coronation?"

Alex's black eyes pinned Dottie's body to the tiles at the edge of the pool. The day after she was leaving Hellenica. "His family has already been invited."

"*My* family?" Mark's eyes had rounded like blue marbles.

"*Yiayia* says we have to be quiet," Zoe warned him.

"I won't talk."

"It's going to be a very great occasion in the cathedral," Dottie explained to him. "Hellenica is going to get a new king. You'll be able to see the crown put on his head."

She nodded. "It gave my *pappou* a headache."

Dottie broke down laughing. Despite the fact that part of her was dying inside, she couldn't hold it back.

"Hey—that's not funny!" Stasio's voice broke in. "Do you know the imperial crown of Hellenica weighs over five pounds? I'll have to wear a five-pound sack of flour on my head the whole day before to get used to it."

"Uncle Stasi!" Zoe called to him in delight and clapped her hands. Dottie hadn't realized he'd come with Alex.

"That's my name." He grinned before doing a belly flop in the pool. The splash got everyone wet. When he came up for air, he looked at the children. "You'd better watch out. I heard there was a shark in here."

"Uh-oh." While the children shrieked, Dottie jumped up. "This is where I opt out."

Without looking back she walked across the tiles to her room. She thought she was alone *until* she saw Alex. He'd followed her dressed in nothing more than his wet black swimming trunks. Dottie's heartbeat switched to hyperspeed. "You're not supposed to be in here. That was our agreement."

He stood there with his hands on his hips. "Last night that agreement was rendered null and void."

"Why?" she whispered in nervous bewilderment.

His eyes narrowed on her features. "You may well ask, but now isn't the time to answer that question. The queen has been sick, but she's starting to feel better and is missing Zoe. I promised to take her back to Hellenica. Stasi has volunteered to babysit the children on the flight while you and I take the cruiser. We'll leave here as soon as you're ready. Pack what you want to take for overnight." On that note, he disappeared.

Dottie gathered up some things, not surprised the queen wanted to see Zoe. It would lift her spirits. Before long they were ready and left with Alex for the dock in the limo. Once on board, he maneuvered the cruiser out of the small bay at a wakeless speed, then opened the throttle and the boat shot ahead.

The helicopter dipped low and circled above them so the children could wave to them. Dottie waved back. She could tell they were having the time of their lives. Alex beeped the horn three times before the helicopter flew on.

"That's precious cargo up there," she told him. "The two little sad sacks of a month ago have undergone a big transformation. I had no idea if the experiment would work, but I honestly think they like each other."

He squinted at her. "You only think?"

"Well, I don't know for sure. Mark might be pretending because he wants to haul off some of those peacock feathers."

Alex's shoulders shook in silent laughter. While his spirits seemed so much improved, she decided to tell him about the email from Dr. Rice.

He nodded. "I was already informed by him."

Naturally he was. She cleared her throat. "Under the circumstances I thought the new therapist could come to Aurum and stay in one of the guest rooms. We'll let Zoe get used to her and I'll involve her in our games."

When Alex didn't respond she got nervous and said, "Mrs. Hawes will have her own techniques to try out on your daughter, of course. By the time of the coronation, they'll be used to each other. I know it will be difficult for Zoe to say goodbye to me, so we need to handle that carefully."

"I agree." He sounded remote. "I'll think on it."

With those few words, Alex remained quiet, but she didn't mind because his mellow mood was so different from the way he'd been, she was able to relax. For a little while she could pretend they were a normal couple out enjoying each other on this glorious blue sea with the same color of sky above them. Despite her aunt's warnings, Dottie still had a tendency to dream forbidden thoughts, if only for the few minutes they had until they reached the shore.

In this halcyon state she noticed him turn his dark head toward her. "After we dock, you're free until this evening. At eight-thirty I'll send for you. In light of Mrs. Hawes's imminent arrival, we'll finalize the termination of your contract tonight. For Zoe's sake it will be best if you don't drop by her suite to say good-night."

The trip between islands hadn't taken long. Dottie

had been given her few minutes of dreaming, but that was all. With one royal pronouncement, even that brief time had been dashed to smithereens.

CHAPTER NINE

TONIGHT was different from all the other nights in Alex's life. As he'd told Dottie last week, he couldn't be in two places at once. In order to help his brother, he'd sent her and Zoe to Aurum. But this night he needed to be alone with the woman who'd turned the lights on for him. Only Dottie had known the location of the secret switch. Through her magic, she'd found it and now no power could turn it off.

After eating dinner with Zoe and putting her to bed, Alex asked his brother to read her some stories until she fell asleep. While he did that, Alex slipped away to shower and dress in a black silk shirt and trousers, just formal enough to let Dottie know what this night meant to him.

He flicked his gaze around the private dining room of his own jet. It was one of the few places where they could have privacy and be secure away from the palace. The steward had set up the preparations for their intimate dinner, complete with flickering candlelight.

Alex had never used his plane for anything but transportation and business meetings. Tonight it would serve as his portal to a future he'd never dared dream about. Now that he could, his body throbbed at every pulse point. When he pulled the phone from his pocket to answer it, his hand trembled.

Hector was outside. He'd brought Dottie to the airport in the limousine. "Tell her to come aboard."

He moved to the entrance of the plane. When she saw him, she paused midway up the steps in a pink-and-white-print dress he hadn't seen before. She looked breathtaking. Her honey blond-hair had been swept into a knot.

Though she'd picked up a golden tan over the past month, she had a noticeable pallor. He hoped to heaven it was because the thought of leaving him was killing her. Maybe it had been cruel to set her up this way, but he'd wanted proof that she couldn't live without him either. If he'd misread the radar...

"Come all the way in, Dottie. I've got dinner waiting for us."

She bit her lower lip. "I couldn't possibly eat, Alex. I'm sorry for any trouble you've gone to. We could have taken care of business in your office."

He lounged against the opening, half surprised at that response. "We could have, but the office is too public a place for the proposal I have in mind."

By the look in her blue eyes, she acted as if she'd just had a dagger plunged into her heart. "There can't be anything but indecent proposals between you and me." Her wintry comment might have frozen him if he didn't know certain things she wasn't aware of yet.

His black brows lifted. "If you'll finish that long walk into the plane, I'll enlighten you about a very decent one you wouldn't have thought of."

She remained where she was. "If you've decided to abandon your family and the monarchy and hide away in some distant place for the rest of your life, then you're not the prince I imagined you to be."

Her answer thrilled him because it meant she'd not only thought of every possibility for finding a way the two of them could be together, she'd actually put voice to it.

"Then you like it that I'm Prince Alexius?"

He could tell she was struggling to pretend her breath hadn't almost left her lungs. "That's an absurd question. You couldn't be anyone else. It's who you are."

"In other words I'm *your* highness, and you're *my* lowness."

She averted her eyes. "Don't joke about serious matters like this."

"Joking is how I've gotten through life this far."

Her head flew back. "That's very tragic. Why did you have me driven here?" she cried. "The truth!"

"Can you stand to hear it?" he fired back in a quiet voice.

"Alex—" She'd dispensed with his title. That was progress.

"I have a plan I want to talk over with you."

He could see her throat working. "What plan? There can be no plan."

"If you'll come aboard, I'll tell you. In case you think I'm going to kidnap you, I swear this jet won't leave the ground. But since I'm a target for the press, who have their Telephoto lenses focused on us as we speak, I'd prefer we talked in private."

He felt her hesitation before she took one step, then another, until she'd entered the plane. His steward closed the door behind them.

"This way." Alex refrained from touching her. The

time wasn't right. As soon as they entered the dining room, he heard her soft cry. She looked at everything as if she was in some sort of daze. He'd been in one since last night.

"Why did you go to all this trouble?"

"Because it occurred to me you've done all the work since you came to Hellenica. I thought you deserved a little fuss to be made over *you* for a change." He held out a chair for her, but she didn't budge.

"Alex—it's *me* you're talking to. Mrs. Richards, the speech therapist. If there are lies between us, then this meeting is pointless. Please stop dancing around the subject. What's the purpose in my coming here?"

"More than you know."

"You're being cryptic. I can't do this." She turned away from him but he caught her arm.

"All I ask is that you hear me out."

The beautiful line of her jaw hardened. "What if I don't want to listen?"

They stood there like adversaries. "I thought that after everything we've been through together, you trusted me. I think you know I trust you with my life, but apparently I've made a mistake about you." Alex took a calculated risk and let go of her hand. "If you don't want anything more to do with me, then you're free to leave now."

Dottie stayed planted to the same spot. Her breathing sounded labored. "Is this about Zoe?"

"About Zoe. About you. About me. If you'll sit down, Hector will explain."

Her eyes widened. "Hector—"

"Yes. I'll phone him now."

The older man had a certain gravitas even Dottie recognized. While she continued to stand where she was, he rang the older man. Within a minute, Hector joined them.

"Your Highness?" He bowed.

"Would you please tell Mrs. Richards what you told me last night?"

"Certainly." Hector cleared his throat and proceeded to explain what Stasio had jokingly said earlier was Alex's get-out-of-jail-free card. "Before Prince Alexius married, his father, King Stefano, knew of Princess Teresa's heart condition and worried about it. Eventually he made a legal proviso that cannot be broken.

"Simply stated, it reads that should she precede him in death and he wishes to marry again, he—who is second in line to the crown—would have the constitutional right to choose his own wife whether she be of royal blood or a commoner. However, any children born of that union would have no claim to the throne."

Alex watched Dottie slowly sink to the chair he'd pulled out for her. When the older man had finished, he thanked him.

"I'm happy to be of service, Your Highness. If you need me, I'll be out in the limo." He exited the plane while Dottie rubbed her arms with her hands, as if she were chilly.

"The gods on Mount Pelos have heard me," Alex began. "Until I met you, Dottie, I never wanted to marry again. And now, thanks to my father, I'm now able to ask you to marry me." He stared at her for a long moment. "I'm making you an honorable, legally binding offer of marriage."

She finally looked at him. The pupils of her eyes had grown so large, she was obviously in shock. "I couldn't be happier that because of your father's intervention, you've suddenly been given your free agency to choose your own wife. For him to think that far ahead for your welfare shows he really did love you. What I don't understand is why didn't Hector come forward ages ago so you could have found someone else by now?"

Alex was thunderstruck by her question. Had his proposal of marriage meant nothing to her?

"Hector didn't tell me why, but I suspect it's because he secretly loves Zoe like his own granddaughter. He never married or had children. I'm convinced that seeing her so happy with you and so unhappy at the prospect of becoming the stepdaughter of Princess Genevieve prompted him to come forward. The queen may have his allegiance, but Zoe has his heart. Hector has seen the three of us together and knows I'll always put my daughter first."

"But you've only known me for a month, Alex! You're *young!* You've got years to find the kind of relationship you've dreamed of having."

He leaned forward. "I've already had years of relationships that filled the loneliness from time to time, but now I have a daughter who's as precious to me as your son was to you. If I'd searched the world over, I couldn't have found the more perfect mother for her than you."

"So that's all you want? A mother?"

"After what we've shared, you know better than to ask me that. I'm in love with you and you know it, but even though you've responded to me physically, I'm aware your heart died when you lost your husband and son. I live in the hope that one day you'll come to love me with the same intensity. As for Zoe, she loves you so much, she was calling you mommy almost from the beginning."

"Yes, but—"

"It would be a second chance for both of us to find happiness," he spoke over her. "We could make a home anywhere you want. If you prefer to stay in New York and further your career, we'll buy a house there. Our home will be our castle."

An incredulous expression broke out on her face. "What are you talking about?"

"What all normal couples talk about when they're discussing marriage. I want you to be happy."

"But your place is here in Hellenica!"

"Listen to me, Dottie. I'll always be Prince Alexius, but I don't have to live here. Not now. Thanks to technology, it won't matter where we settle down because I can do my mining engineering work anywhere."

"Be serious—your family and friends are here!"

"Yes, and we'll come for visits."

"I'm talking about your life!"

"My life will be with my own little family. You have no idea how much I want to take care of you. I love you. You'll be my first priority."

"You think the queen is going to stand for that?" She sounded frightened.

"She has no say in this matter."

"You're really serious, aren't you?"

"Of course."

In the quiet that followed, Dottie stared into the candle flames. "I feel like I'm in some kind of strange dream. What if I didn't exist?" she cried out. "What would you be planning to do with this new freedom?"

It appeared he was wrong about her feelings. The

knowledge that they could be together legitimately hadn't changed anything for her.

"It's a moot point. You *do* exist, and you've won Hector around, otherwise he would never have come forward with that document." At this point Alex couldn't comprehend life without her, but maybe he'd been mistaken in thinking there was a future for them. "After the coronation, I plan to live with Zoe on Aurum as always. Shall I consider this your answer?"

When she didn't say anything, Alex's burgeoning hopes disintegrated into blackness. He pushed himself away from the table and got to his feet. "If you're ready to leave, I'll walk you out to the limo and Hector will see you get back to the palace."

Once she'd said good-night to Hector, Dottie hurried to her room so torn up inside she didn't know how she was going to make it through the night. Alex's marriage proposal had turned her world upside down.

He'd told her he'd fallen in love with her, but that had to be his desire talking. She knew he desired her, but feared it would eventually wear off now that she was no longer forbidden fruit. If they married and then he grew tired of her, she couldn't bear it.

She still couldn't comprehend that one minute he was doomed to the life he'd been born into, and the next minute he was free to take a commoner for his wife. It was too convenient. If she hadn't heard it from his own lips—from Hector's—she wouldn't have believed it, not in a million years.

Didn't he realize he could marry any woman he wanted? The idea that he'd move to New York for her was a pipe dream. You didn't take the prince out of the man no matter how hard you tried. She didn't want to do that to him. She loved Alex for who he was, but she wasn't about to ruin his life by condemning him to another prison.

Dottie was painfully in love with him, but she wasn't his grand passion. Once his gratitude to her wore off, he'd want his freedom. She couldn't handle that. It was better to remain single and just do her job. The time had come for her to watch out for herself and what she wanted.

Full of adrenaline, she went to the closet for her luggage and started packing. Mrs. Hawes would be on the job in the morning. Zoe wouldn't be happy about it, but in time she'd adjust. Her speech was improving every day. She was already getting some self-confidence. Alex would keep working with her.

As Dottie cleaned out the schoolroom, she kept telling herself Zoe was going to be fine. She and her daddy had each other. That was the important thing. After another hour she had everything packed and finally crawled into bed, praying for sleep to come. But her pillow was wet before oblivion took over.

The next time she had cognizance of her surroundings, she heard a child crying. The sound tugged at her deepest emotions.

"Cory?" she murmured. Her eyes opened.

"Dot," a voice called out her name clearly in the early morning light. It was Zoe! "Dot?"

"I'm right here."

"Mommy," she cried her other name for her and climbed onto the bed.

Dottie pulled her close and rocked her in her arms. "Did you have a bad dream?"

"No. *Yiayia* says a new teacher has come to help me. Don't go, Mommy. Don't go." Her little body shook from her tears. She clung to Dottie.

"Shh. It's all right." Dottie kissed her wet eyes and cheeks. Her dear little face was flushed. She sang some songs she used to sing to Cory. After a few minutes Zoe started to quiet down. Just when it appeared she'd fallen asleep and Dottie could alert the staff, the palace phone rang, startling both of them.

Zoe lifted her head. "I want to stay here."

Dottie reached for the receiver and said hello.

"Dottie—" The anxiety in Alex's voice was that of any frantic parent who couldn't find his child.

"Zoe's with me. I was just going to let you know."

"Thank heaven. I'll be right there."

Alex must have broken the speed record. By the time she'd thrown on her robe, he'd entered her bedroom out of breath and looking so pale it worried her. He was still dressed in the stunning black silk shirt and trousers he'd worn on the jet. It meant he'd been up all night, which made her feel so guilty she wanted to die.

Zoe stood up in the bed. "Don't be mad, Daddy."

A sound of anguish escaped his throat as he reached for her and hugged her tight. "I went to your room to kiss you good morning, but you weren't there."

"I know. I came to see Dot."

"How did you get past the guards?"

"I ran when they didn't see me."

Dottie heard his groan. "You gave me a fright."

"*Yiayia* said I have a new teacher and Dot is leaving. I don't want a new teacher. Please don't let Dot leave—" The pain in her voice was too much for Dottie, who couldn't stop her own tears.

"I can't make Dottie stay, Zoe." The sound that came out of him seeped from a new level of sadness and despair, finding a responding chord in her.

"Yes, you can," Zoe fought her father.

He shook his dark head and kissed her curls. "You're going to learn you can't force people to do things they don't want to do. Come on. Let's take a walk on the beach and then we'll have breakfast."

"No—" she screamed as he started to carry her out. Still in his arms, Zoe turned her head to look at Dottie. "Don't leave, Mommy. I don't want to go. Stop, Daddy—"

Dottie had a vision of them walking out that door. What if she never saw them again? The day of the car accident Neil had grabbed Cory to take him on an errand. Both of them were smiling as he carried their son out the front door. Dottie never saw them alive again.

The thought of never seeing Alex or Zoe again was unthinkable.

"Wait, Alex—"

He'd already started out the door. The momentum caused him to take a few more steps before he swung around. His haunted expression tore her heart to shreds.

"You really want to marry me?" she whispered shakily.

He slowly lowered Zoe to the marble floor and started toward her. "Would I have asked, otherwise?"

It was the moment of truth. She had to have faith that their marriage could work. He'd told her he loved her. He was willing to move to New York, willing to give her the opportunity of loving his wonderful daughter. What more could a woman ask?

But she'd been thinking about it all night. Her deepest fear was that this royal prince, who'd been denied the possibility of a happy marriage the first time, was jumping impulsively into another marriage he'd regret down the road. He was a free man. If he chose to, he could go where he wanted and live like a commoner with another woman.

After what had happened to Neil and Cory, Dottie wanted a guarantee of happiness. But as her aunt had told her, there were no guarantees. *You're a romantic, Dottie. For that reason you can be hurt the worst. Why set yourself up, honey?*

Her aunt's advice had come too late. For better or worse, Dottie *had* set herself up.

She closed the distance between them. "I love you, Alex. So much, you have no idea." Emotion was almost choking her. "I want to be your wife more than anything in the world."

"Darling—" He crushed her to him, wrapping his arms all the way around her. "I adore you, Dottie. I was up all night plotting how to get you to love me," he whispered against her lips before kissing her long and hard. "We need to get married right away."

"I agree," she cried, kissing him back hungrily. "I think we'd better tell Zoe."

"You think?" His smile lit up her insides before he said, "Why don't we do it right here in the alcove."

His arms reluctantly let her go before he drew Zoe over to the table where they'd spent so many delightful times together. Still trembling from the look he'd just given her, Dottie took her place across from them, her usual teacher position. She checked her watch. It was ten to seven in the morning.

Zoe eyed both of them curiously. She'd seen them

kissing and knew something was going on. "Are we going to have school *now*?"

Alex's lips twitched that way they sometimes did when he was trying to hold back his laughter. When he did that, Dottie thought there could be no more attractive man on earth.

"No," he answered. "This morning is a very special morning and we have plans to make because Dottie has just said she would marry me."

The sweetest smile broke out on Zoe's face. "Then you're going to be my real mommy, like Mark's?"

"Yes." Dottie reached across the table to squeeze her hands.

"They're going to have a baby. Mark told me."

"I didn't know that," he answered, trying to keep a deadpan face. Dottie wasn't as successful.

"Can we have one, too?"

Dottie laughed through the tears. "For now you have Baby Betty."

Alex's dark eyes swerved to hers. The look of desire in them took her breath. "If the gods on Mount Pelos are kind, maybe a new baby will come."

Zoe beamed. "A big boy like you, Daddy!"

He trapped Dottie's gaze midair. Her soon-to-be daughter was precocious to a fault, just like her father. Both of them were remembering the jump-rope game. It was the day she fell so hard for Prince Alexius, she hadn't been the same since. She didn't know which moment was the most surreal. But one thing was absolutely certain. She'd committed herself and there was no going back now.

"I tell you what," Alex said. "Let's all get dressed

and have breakfast in my suite while we make plans. After that we'll tell the family."

Zoe stared at her father before giving him a huge kiss. Then she got down and ran around the table to hug Dottie. "I love you, Mommy."

"I love you, too." Over her brown curls she looked at the man she'd just told she was going to marry. "I love you both beyond belief."

Dottie had been to Alex's apartment once before, but her thoughts had been so focused on her diagnostic session with Zoe, she hadn't really looked around and appreciated the magnificence of her surroundings.

During their fabulous breakfast out on the patio, a delivery came for Dottie. She opened the long florist box and discovered two dozen long-stemmed red roses with the most heavenly fragrance. The little card said, *For the first time in my life, I feel like a king whose every wish has come true.* Coming from Alex, those words had unique significance.

After kissing Dottie hungrily, he excused himself to go visit his grandmother and make sure she was up. He told Dottie and Zoe he'd be coming by for them in a few minutes, at which point they would go to the queen's drawing room and tell her their news.

After Stasio had refused to marry Princess Beatriz, Alex's announcement was going to be another terrible disappointment. Dottie feared it might be too much for Zoe's *yiayia* and she would suffer from something worse than ulcers. In a way Dottie had it in her heart to feel sorry for the dowager whose world was crumbling before her very eyes.

The older woman had grown up knowing nothing

but her duty. Somehow she had made her own marriage work, and so had Alex's parents. Deep down it had to be very hard on her to see her two wonderful grandsons so terribly unhappy up to now.

Dottie played with Zoe out on the patio, but she kept waiting for Alex to appear. A maid brought them some much-appreciated refreshments. Dottie asked for a vase so she could put the gorgeous roses in water. The gesture from Alex was one of the reasons she loved him so much.

After being in the apartment for two hours with no word from him, she started to get nervous. Perhaps his grandmother had suffered a setback from the news. He and Stasio were probably sequestered with her because Alex's news had shattered another dream. Twice Dottie started to pick up the palace phone and ask to speak to him, then thought the better of it.

Zoe seemed perfectly content to play with her toys, but Dottie was turning into a mass of nerves. Another hour went by, still no word about anything. When 7:00 p.m. rolled around, their dinner was brought in, but no news from Alex. When she didn't think she could stand it a second longer, Hector appeared on the patio where they'd started to eat.

"If I might speak to you in private."

Thank goodness. "I'll be right back, Zoe. I'm just going to the living room."

"Okay."

Dottie followed him into the other room. "Obviously something's wrong. It's been ten hours since Alex told me he'd be back."

"He had to fly to Zurich today and might not return until morning."

She blinked. "As in Switzerland?"

"Yes. He asked me to assure you that he would never have left you and the little princess unless it was an emergency. He would like you to stay in his suite."

No doubt Alex had told him they were getting married. "Then we will."

Hector knew what the emergency was, but he would never tell Dottie. Whatever was going on had to be serious for Alex to go away today. She rubbed her arms nervously. "Is he all right?"

The slight hesitation before he said, "Of course," spoke volumes. "If there's anything else you need, you only have to ask."

"We're fine, Hector. Thank you for telling me. Good night."

"Good night."

Hector was always perfectly correct. He'd served the monarchy all his adult life. Like the queen, he didn't deviate from his role. It would be too much to ask of anyone. She thought of Alex who'd told her he would live in New York if she wanted. She had no doubt he could do it and make the most of it, but he'd been raised a prince. That would never change.

Full of musings, she walked out to the patio. "Zoe?"

"Did Daddy come?"

"Not yet. Something came up."

"I know. It's business."

Dottie smiled. Just then Zoe sounded a hundred years old. "Why don't we get you in the tub for a nice bath, then I'll read you some stories."

"Are we going to sleep in Daddy's bed?"

"Yes. At least until he calls or comes."

A little sound of happiness escaped the little girl's lips.

Dottie rang for a maid to bring them some things from their rooms. Within the hour both of them were ready for bed. Zoe picked out the stories she wanted and they climbed under the covers. Dottie looked around the sumptuous room, hardly able to believe she would be marrying the man who slept in this royal bedchamber when he was on Hellenica.

Though she was filled with anxiety over the reason for Alex's absence, the feel of the warm little body nestled against her brought a comfort to her heart she hadn't known in years. When they read the last book, she kissed her. "I'm so thankful you're going to be my daughter soon. I love you, Zoe."

"I love you. Good night, Mommy."

No one slept more peacefully than a child who wasn't worried about anything. Zoe had her new mommy-to-be, her daddy and her Baby Betty. Her world was complete. Dottie wished she could say the same for herself, but without Alex here to tell her what was going on, she was too anxious to sleep.

Instead of lying there tortured by fears she couldn't even identify, she slid out of bed and threw on her robe. Zoe preferred the patio to any other place in the palace. Dottie was drawn to it, too, and wandered out there where she wouldn't disturb Zoe with her restlessness.

CHAPTER TEN

At one in the morning, Alex stepped off his jet into the limo and headed for the palace. He'd been prepared to stay all night in Valleder with Philippe and Stasio, but both men urged him to go back to Hellenica and be with Dottie and Zoe.

There was nothing Alex wanted so much in this life, but since the last time he'd seen Dottie, his entire world had changed. He couldn't reverse time and put it back to the way it was before he'd gone to his grandmother's apartment to let her know he'd returned from Aurum.

He said good-night to Hector, then entered the palace and went straight to his apartment. But he was so torn up in his soul by the events of the past fifteen hours, the burden of what he had to tell Dottie made his limbs heavy. He felt like an old man as he continued up the steps and down the hall to his suite.

No lights had been left on. The place was quiet as a tomb. He tiptoed to the bedroom and was surprised to see Zoe asleep alone. Instinct told him Dottie was out on the patio and he headed for it.

His thoughts flew back to that first day. He'd walked Zoe out there to be tested. When Dottie had thrown him that Ping-Pong ball, she'd set an energy in motion that had turned him into a different man. Now all the dynamics were different because Mrs. Dottie Richards had agreed to become Mrs. Dottie Constantinides. Or so she'd thought.

This happened to be his favorite time of night, when the moon was on the rise over the Aegean. It was the time when the heat of the day released the perfume from the jasmine, filling the warm air with its heavenly scent. Instead of it being day, this was the night of his engagement. It was a singular irony that his daughter occupied his bed.

He stepped out on the patio and glimpsed his bride-to-be at the other end. His pounding heart almost suffocated him as he moved toward her. She stood at the wall and had put her hands on either side of the ledge, taking in the unparalleled view etched in his mind from childhood. With her standing there, a new softly rounded, feminine sculpture had been added to the landscape.

"Dottie?" he murmured. A cry escaped her lips. She turned toward him in surprise. "Enjoying the view?"

"This kind of beauty goes beyond perfection."

He sucked in his breath. "It does now." She looked gorgeous yet maidenlike standing there in the moonlight in her simple pink robe. Alex found it hard to believe she'd given birth to a child in another time and place.

"Hector said you might not be home before morning."

"I thought I might have to stay in Valleder until tomorrow, but my brother and Philippe sent me back."

Her eyes searched his. "Why did you have to go to Philippe's? What's happened?"

"You deserve a full explanation and you're going to

get one, but it's going to take a while. Maybe you should sit down."

"That sounded ominous." Her voice trembled. "I think I'd prefer to stand."

"The bottom line is, Stasio submitted papers to the ministers and has taken the steps to abdicate from the monarchy."

In the silence that followed, he watched her face pale. "*What* did you say?"

"Apparently he's been planning it for a long time. When you suggested that I might have decided to abdicate in order to marry you, the idea wasn't so far-fetched after all. You just happened to apply it to the wrong prince."

A hand went to her throat. "He's really stepping down?"

"Yes. After Stasi called off his betrothal, I should have guessed this would be the next step, but I've been so caught up in my feelings for you, I'm not the same person anymore."

"Darling..."

"It's true, Dottie. The reason he was out of the country so long was because he had to work things out with Philippe."

"What things?"

"Stasi has persuaded our second cousin to rule as king over Hellenica."

She shook her head. "I don't believe it."

"Philippe will be able to reign over both countries without problem. The Houses of Valleder and Constantinides are intrinsically entwined. He's well loved in Valleder. It will be the same here."

She looked shellshocked. "Aren't *you* the second in line to the throne?"

"Yes. But Stasio knows how I feel and would never put me in that position, especially now that I'm going to marry you and move to New York. Zoe is third in line and, if she wishes, will rule one day when Philippe is no longer king."

"So does that mean the coronation has been called off?"

"Yes. The announcement will go out on the news to-morrow evening. My grandmother will continue to be the head of the monarchy until Philippe is installed."

Dottie stared out at the sea. "I'm surprised the queen isn't in the hospital by now."

"She may end up there, but she hasn't given up the fight yet. This change to install Philippe has to be voted on by the ministers of the parliament. She has power-ful friends there. So does Stasi. I believe the votes for Philippe will prevail. She's calling for an emergency assembly."

"What if they vote against installing your cousin?"

"Then she'll continue to reign until her death, issu-ing her edicts through the head of parliament."

"And after that?"

"The parliament will convene to find an heir from the Constantinides line. We have a fourth cousin living on the island of Cuprum in the Thracian Sea. He's in his sixties and could be brought up for consideration. However, we have no idea how long my grandmother will live. She has a strong constitution and could out-live him."

"This is all so unbelievable. Your poor grandmother.

Poor Stasio," she whispered, wringing her hands. "To be so desperate for his freedom, he'd give up everything..."

"Actually, I never saw anyone happier than he was when I left him. He's been in love with a woman from Norway for the past ten years and had to make a choice. In the end he chose Solveig. He's a different man now."

"I can only imagine. The second you said abdicate, I thought there had to be a woman. Only a powerful love could cause him to make a break with your family."

"I told him he was insane if he ever wasted another moment feeling guilty about what he's done."

"You're a wonderful brother to say that to him."

"Stasi would do the same for me. Fortunately our father provided that escape clause for me in his will. Otherwise there would have been two abdications."

"You don't really mean that." Her voice shook.

He gave an elegant shrug of his shoulders. "After Teresa died, I put the idea of marriage completely out of my mind. Much later I realized I wanted to marry you, and knew I would have to have papers drawn up for my abdication because there was no way I was going to let you get away from me. I loved you from the moment I saw you. When Hector heard you were leaving, he acted on my father's wishes and told me about the codicil to his will. As you said, it takes a powerful love."

Her breathing had changed. "You loved me from the beginning?"

"I realize now that I fell for you the moment you walked into my office and treated me like an ordinary man. You had no idea what that did to me. My world changed and I knew I had to have you, even if it meant turning my back on my heritage."

"Alex—

"I love you desperately. When we reach New York, I plan to show you what you mean to me. I'll do whatever I have to in order to make our marriage work."

"So will I," she declared. "Don't you know I'm so crazy about you, I'd do anything for you, too? At first I feared the only reason you wanted to marry me was because I was forbidden fruit and able to be a mother figure for Zoe. But I took the risk and said yes to you anyway because I'm so in love with you, nothing else matters."

"Do you have any concept of what those words mean to me, Dottie? I raced back here from Valleder fearing maybe all this was a fantastic dream. It's so hard to believe that I've found the only woman for me, and she loves me, too."

"Then believe this—I don't want to go back to New York with you. I don't want to live there."

"Of course you do. It's your home."

"It was once, but then I came to your world and I've grown to love it here. *You're* here. I would never expect you to cast aside your whole way of life for me. Being Zoe's therapist has brought me smack-dab into the heart of your world. I've learned so much and I'm still learning."

The blood was pounding in his ears. "You're just saying this because it's what you think I want to hear."

"Well, isn't it? Besides the fact that what I'm telling you is true, what do you think those wedding vows are going to be about? I plan to love, honor and serve you through the good and the bad. This is a bad time for your family. Without Stasio, you need me to help you keep the monarchy together.

"Your grandmother needs you. Even though I haven't

met her, I like her, Alex. I really do. She has tried to do her duty the way she's seen fit and Zoe adores her. Why should King Philippe or any other royal family member have to be brought in when you're the son meant to take up the reins? I believe your father knew that."

Alex couldn't believe what he was hearing.

"Alex, you've already been carrying a lot of the load your whole life. Stasio tried his best to shield you by turning to Philippe. He did everything in his power to help you, but you don't need his help.

"I've watched and listened. Your marriage to Teresa proves to me you cared more for the kingdom than you know, or like Stasio you would have abdicated a long time ago. To my mind, you were born to be king. Your country means everything to you, otherwise you wouldn't have agreed to serve in Stasio's place while he's been away. I love you, Alex. I revere you for wanting to do the noble thing and I love the idea of helping you."

Her brilliant blue eyes flashed like the sapphire of the ring he hadn't given her yet. It was still in his suite on Aurum. Those eyes let him know the truth. It was pouring from her soul. "All you have to do is turn around and accept the crown, my love."

There was a swelling in his chest that felt as though it might be a heart attack.

"You and I will always have each other and you and Stasio will be able to live without any guilt. He can marry the woman he loves. They can come and visit, have children, give Zoe a cousin or two. Hector will be thrilled. The queen can take a well-earned rest and Zoe will always be our darling girl. It's the best of all worlds."

Her logic moved him to tears, but he shook his head. "You don't understand. I can't rule with a commoner for a wife, and I refuse to give you up."

"Who says you can't?" she shot back. "I didn't hear about that when Hector explained the contents of your father's codicil to me. It only said that if we have a child or children together, they won't have claim to the throne. That will be Zoe's privilege."

Alex rubbed the back of his neck. "Everything you've said makes perfect sense, but it's never been done."

"That still doesn't make it impossible. Let's go to the queen right now. Wake her up if you have to and tell her you're willing to rule Hellenica with me at your side. Since your father broke the rules when he made that extension to his will, it stands to reason his mother could be moved to convince the ministers to vote in our favor for the good of the monarchy.

"There's no one who can do greater good for the country than you, Alex. You've already been running everything singlehandedly and doing a brilliant job. Maybe it was a presentiment on my part, but the night of the party I watched you and thought you should be king, not Stasio."

In the next instant he reached blindly for her. "You don't know what you're saying."

"I think I do." She clutched his arms. "All I need to know is one thing. Look me in the eye and tell me you don't want to salvage the House of Constantinides. If you're not truthful with me now, then the marriage we're about to enter into is a sham and won't last."

He crushed her in his arms, rocking her long and hard. With his face buried in her hair he whispered, "What have I ever done to deserve you?"

"It'll take me a lifetime to tell you everything, but first we have to tell the queen. Phone your grandmother now. She needs help. Who better than the father of her beloved Zoe?"

Alex kissed the side of her neck. "Whether or not I become king—whether or not my grandmother decides she wants us to have a public wedding here on Hellenica at the time of the coronation—it doesn't matter as long as for once in my life I do get to do the thing I thought I'd never be able to do."

"What's that?" Dottie asked breathlessly.

He cupped her face in his hands. "Marry the woman of my dreams in the chapel on Aurum tomorrow."

"Alex—"

"It will be a very private ceremony just for us. The tiny church located on the palace grounds isn't open to the public. It was erected for the family's use. Father Gregorius will marry us. I'll ask him to perform the ceremony in English."

"He doesn't have to go to that trouble."

"Yes, he does. I'm marrying the bride of my heart and want to say my vows in English for your sake. My friend Bari will be our witness along with Inez and Ari. And, of course, Zoe."

Dottie clung to Alex's hand as he escorted her and Zoe inside the dark interior of the church that smelled strongly of beeswax candles and incense. She wore her white dress with the yellow sash. Dottie had dressed in the pink print and had left her hair down because Zoe had told her earlier that her daddy loved her hair like that.

Inez stepped forward. She handed Dottie a bouquet

of cornflowers. Against Dottie's ear Alex whispered, "I asked her to gather these this morning. They match the incredible blue of your eyes."

She felt tears start and soon saw that another, smaller bouquet had been picked for Zoe to hold. Alex was wearing a light blue summer suit. After putting two cornflowers inside his lapel, he led her and Zoe to the front where the priest stood at the altar. Inez beckoned Zoe to stand by her.

Despite the fact that Alex would always be a prince, Dottie realized he'd dispensed with all artifice for their wedding. She knew the last thing he wanted was for her to feel overwhelmed. Her heart quivered with her love for him as the ceremony began.

"Do you, Prince Alexius Kristof Rudolph Stefano Valleder Constantinides, Duke of Aurum, take Dorothy Giles Richards to be thy wedded wife? To love, honor and serve her unto death?"

"I do."

Dottie trembled.

"Do you, Dorothy Giles Richards, take Prince Alexius to be thy wedded husband? To love, honor and serve him unto death?"

"I do," she whispered, scarcely able to believe this was really happening.

"Then by the power invested in me, I proclaim you husband and wife from this day forth. What God has blessed, let no man put asunder. In the name of the Trinity, Amen."

"Amen," Alex declared after Dottie spoke.

"You wish to bestow tokens?"

"I do, Father." He reached for Dottie's left hand and slid the one-carat sapphire onto her ring finger.

"You may kiss your bride."

The significance of this moment shook Dottie to her very roots. Alex was her husband now. Her life! Without caring about anything else, she raised her mouth to his, needing his kiss like she needed the sun on her face and air to breathe.

While they stood locked together, Zoe ran over to them and hugged their legs. She felt her little arms, reminding her she and Alex were probably giving Father Gregorius a coronary for letting their kiss go on so long. No doubt she was blushing, but the others wouldn't be able to tell until they went outside.

"Are you married now, Daddy?"

Alex relinquished Dottie's mouth and picked up his daughter to kiss her. "We're very, very married."

She giggled and turned to reach for Dottie, who hugged her.

Bari stepped forward and gave Alex a bear hug before bestowing a kiss on Dottie's cheek.

"Congratulations, Your Highness." Inez and Ari curtsied to him and Dottie, then handed her the bouquet. "Your Highness."

"Thank you," Dottie answered.

Alex shook their hands. "We appreciate all your help."

"It's been our pleasure."

"Let's go outside for some pictures," Bari suggested.

The priest stayed long enough for a group photo in front of the ancient doors, then he had to be on his way to the city. Alex invited Bari to have a drink with them. At Zoe's suggestion they celebrated in the gazebo. Bari drank to their health and happiness. After one more picture, he left to get back to work.

Inez brought out a tray of salad, sandwiches and a pitcher of iced tea. By now they were all hungry, including Zoe. A month ago her appetite had diminished to the point they'd both worried about it, but no longer.

The peacock happened to walk past the gazebo just then. Zoe scrambled out of her chair and went after it, leaving them alone for a minute. Alex caught her in his arms. "Alone at last. Happy wedding day, Mrs. Constantinides."

"I love you, darling," she blurted. "Thank you for the simple, beautiful ceremony. I loved it. I love my ring. I'll treasure this day forever. I'm only sorry I didn't have a ring for you."

He kissed her passionately on the mouth. "I didn't want one. I don't like rings and would prefer not to wear one. Yet I have seven of them, all with precious gems encrusted. The only one that doesn't have stones is this one." He flexed his right hand where he wore the gold ducal crest. "Since I have to wear it, I'll take it off and let you put it on the ring finger of my left hand."

He removed it and handed it to her.

At first she was all thumbs. Finally she took hold of his hand and slid it home. "Did you wear it on this hand when you were married to Zoe's mother?" she asked without looking at him.

"No. She gave me a ring from the House of Valleder. I took it off after she died and put it with the other rings that Zoe will inherit one day."

As she stared into his eyes, she sensed something else was on his mind. "You have news. I can tell."

"Yes. For one thing, Hector explained the situation to Mrs. Hawes and she's been given a free two-week vacation here if she wants. Now you don't have to worry about her needless trip."

"Oh, thank you, darling. That's so generous of you."

"After meeting you, I realized how hard-working and dedicated you therapists are. She deserves every perk we can offer."

Dottie bit her lip. "What else were you going to tell me?"

His expression grew more solemn. She saw the slightest look of vulnerability in his eyes. "Before we left Hellenica this morning, my grandmother told me the vote from the parliament was unanimous. They want me to be king. So does she."

His news was so wonderful, she threw her arms around his neck. "You're going to be the greatest king this country ever had. I'm the luckiest woman in the world because I'm your wife. I promise to help make your life easier. I swear it."

"Dottie—" He pulled her tightly against him. "You realize what this means. The day after tomorrow will be my coronation. The queen wants us to come to the palace immediately to discuss the arrangements for our wedding. We're going to have to go through another ceremony, and then I will be crowned king. She wants to meet the commoner who stole the hearts of her great-granddaughter and grandson."

This time tears rolled down Dottie's cheeks. She grasped his handsome face in her hands. "I can't wait to meet her. I can't wait to say my vows again. I love you," she cried, covering his face with kisses.

The archbishop of Hellenica closed the coronation ceremony with "God Save the King." Dottie adored this great man she'd just married for the second time. He'd now been crowned king in this magnificent cathedral and was so handsome and splendid in his dark blue ceremonial suit and red sash, it hurt to look at him.

Zoe, dressed in a tiara and frilly white floor-length dress, sat on a velvet chair like a perfect little princess between Dottie and her great-grandmother, who'd come in a wheelchair. Stasio sat opposite them in his ceremonial dress. Solveig, the woman he loved, had come and was seated in the crowd. Dottie liked her already and imagined there'd be a wedding soon.

King Philippe and his pregnant American wife sat next to Stasio. Over the past few days Dottie had gotten to know her and couldn't wait to spend more time with her.

When the archbishop bid Princess Dorothy rise to join Alex for the processional out of the church, Dottie realized it was *she* he meant and blushed like mad. Her husband noticed she'd been caught off guard and his black eyes flashed fire as she walked toward him to grasp his hand. Zoe followed to carry the train.

In an intimate appraisal, his gaze swept from the tiara on top of her white lace mantilla, down her white princess-style wedding gown to her satin slippers. He'd given her that same look as she'd started to get out of bed this morning. When she reminded him they should have been up an hour ago, he'd pulled her back on top of him and made love to her again with insatiable hunger.

It was embarrassing how much time they'd spent in the bedroom when there was so much to get done in preparation for the coronation. But obviously not embarrassing enough, because she was the one who always moaned in protest when Hector finally managed to convince Alex he was needed in the office or the queen's drawing room immediately.

Her husband kept squeezing her hand as they slowly made their way toward the great doors. In her heart she knew that if Neil and Cory were looking on, they would be happy for her.

She smiled at the guests standing on either side of the aisle. Everyone looked wonderful in their hats and wedding finery. Halfway down she caught sight of Mark and his parents. He made a little wave to Dottie and Zoe with his hand. It warmed her heart. Next she smiled at Bari and his family. Near the doors she spotted Hector, who beamed back at her.

When she and Alex emerged from the cathedral, a huge roar went up from the crowd in the ancient agora. Alex helped her into the open-air carriage, then assisted Zoe, who sat opposite them. Once he'd climbed inside and closed the door, the bells began to ring throughout the city.

Almost at once a chant went through the crowd for King Alexius to kiss Princess Dot. Somehow word had gotten out that Princess Zoe called her new mother Dot.

"Don't mind if I do," Alex said with a wicked smile before he kissed her so thoroughly her tiara slipped off. The crowd went wild with excitement. The horses began moving.

While Alex fit it back on her, taking his time about it as he stared at her, Zoe said, "Was the crown heavy, Daddy?"

"Very. Your Uncle Stasi wasn't kidding."

"Could Mark ride with us, Mommy?"

"Not today, but you'll see him tomorrow. There are hundreds of children lining the streets with their families. They'd all love to ride in this carriage with you, so wave to them. They're very excited to see you."

"They are?"

"Yes. Just think—today your country got a new king and he's *your* daddy. We need to start working on your K sounds."

Alex's chuckle turned into a deep rumble. He leaned over to give her another kiss that stirred her senses clear down to her toenails. It was a kiss that told her he couldn't wait until they were alone again. As they reached the palace and climbed out of the carriage, the limo carrying the queen and Stasio pulled up behind them.

As they all entered the palace together, Alex's grandmother said, "Really, Alex. Did you have to kiss Dottie like that in front of thousands of people? And you kept doing it! You realize it'll be all over the news."

He grinned at Stasio. "I don't know how to kiss her any other way, *Yiayia*. Worse, I can't seem to stop."

"Are we going to have a baby now?" piped up a little voice.

"Oh, really, Zoe!" her great-grandmother cried out. "You don't ask questions like that in front of people. There's going to be a reception in the grand dining hall and I expect you to behave like the princess you are."

Unabashed, Zoe turned to Hector. "Can Mark sit by me?"

While they were sorting it out, Alex pulled Dottie away from the others and led her to a deserted alcove. Before she could breathe, he kissed her long and deeply. "I needed that," he murmured after lifting his head a few minutes later. "You looked like a vision in the cathedral. Promise me you're not a figment of my imagination. I couldn't take it."

She kissed his hard jaw. "I'll convince you tonight when we're finally alone. I'm so glad I married royalty. I love the idea of going to bed with my husband and *my liege*. It sounds positively decadent and wicked, don't you think?"

"Dottie—"

* * * * *

Mills & Boon® Hardback

March 2012

ROMANCE

Roccanti's Marriage Revenge	Lynne Graham
The Devil and Miss Jones	Kate Walker
Sheikh Without a Heart	Sandra Marton
Savas's Wildcat	Anne McAllister
The Argentinian's Solace	Susan Stephens
A Wicked Persuasion	Catherine George
Girl on a Diamond Pedestal	Maisey Yates
The Theotokis Inheritance	Susanne James
The Good, the Bad and the Wild	Heidi Rice
The Ex Who Hired Her	Kate Hardy
A Bride for the Island Prince	Rebecca Winters
Pregnant with the Prince's Child	Raye Morgan
The Nanny and the Boss's Twins	Barbara McMahon
Once a Cowboy...	Patricia Thayer
Mr Right at the Wrong Time	Nikki Logan
When Chocolate Is Not Enough...	Nina Harrington
Sydney Harbour Hospital: Luca's Bad Girl	Amy Andrews
Falling for the Sheikh She Shouldn't	Fiona McArthur

HISTORICAL

Untamed Rogue, Scandalous Mistress	Bronwyn Scott
Honourable Doctor, Improper Arrangement	Mary Nichols
The Earl Plays With Fire	Isabelle Goddard
His Border Bride	Blythe Gifford

MEDICAL

Dr Cinderella's Midnight Fling	Kate Hardy
Brought Together by Baby	Margaret McDonagh
The Firebrand Who Unlocked His Heart	Anne Fraser
One Month to Become a Mum	Louisa George

ROMANCE

The Power of Vasilii	Penny Jordan
The Real Rio D'Aquila	Sandra Marton
A Shameful Consequence	Carol Marinelli
A Dangerous Infatuation	Chantelle Shaw
How a Cowboy Stole Her Heart	Donna Alward
Tall, Dark, Texas Ranger	Patricia Thayer
The Boy is Back in Town	Nina Harrington
Just An Ordinary Girl?	Jackie Braun

HISTORICAL

The Lady Gambles	Carole Mortimer
Lady Rosabella's Ruse	Ann Lethbridge
The Viscount's Scandalous Return	Anne Ashley
The Viking's Touch	Joanna Fulford

MEDICAL

Cort Mason – Dr Delectable	Carol Marinelli
Survival Guide to Dating Your Boss	Fiona McArthur
Return of the Maverick	Sue MacKay
It Started with a Pregnancy	Scarlet Wilson
Italian Doctor, No Strings Attached	Kate Hardy
Miracle Times Two	Josie Metcalfe

Mills & Boon® Hardback
April 2012

ROMANCE

A Deal at the Altar	Lynne Graham
Return of the Moralis Wife	Jacqueline Baird
Gianni's Pride	Kim Lawrence
Undone by his Touch	Annie West
The Legend of de Marco	Abby Green
Stepping out of the Shadows	Robyn Donald
Deserving of his Diamonds?	Melanie Milburne
Girl Behind the Scandalous Reputation	Michelle Conder
Redemption of a Hollywood Starlet	Kimberly Lang
Cracking the Dating Code	Kelly Hunter
The Cattle King's Bride	Margaret Way
Inherited: Expectant Cinderella	Myrna Mackenzie
The Man Who Saw Her Beauty	Michelle Douglas
The Last Real Cowboy	Donna Alward
New York's Finest Rebel	Trish Wylie
The Fiancée Fiasco	Jackie Braun
Sydney Harbour Hospital: Tom's Redemption	Fiona Lowe
Summer With A French Surgeon	Margaret Barker

HISTORICAL

Dangerous Lord, Innocent Governess	Christine Merrill
Captured for the Captain's Pleasure	Ann Lethbridge
Brushed by Scandal	Gail Whitiker
Lord Libertine	Gail Ranstrom

MEDICAL

Georgie's Big Greek Wedding?	Emily Forbes
The Nurse's Not-So-Secret Scandal	Wendy S. Marcus
Dr Right All Along	Joanna Neil
Doctor on Her Doorstep	Annie Claydon

0312 GEN STD HB

Mills & Boon® Large Print
April 2012

ROMANCE

Jewel in His Crown	Lynne Graham
The Man Every Woman Wants	Miranda Lee
Once a Ferrara Wife...	Sarah Morgan
Not Fit for a King?	Jane Porter
Snowbound with Her Hero	Rebecca Winters
Flirting with Italian	Liz Fielding
Firefighter Under the Mistletoe	Melissa McClone
The Tycoon Who Healed Her Heart	Melissa James

HISTORICAL

The Lady Forfeits	Carole Mortimer
Valiant Soldier, Beautiful Enemy	Diane Gaston
Winning the War Hero's Heart	Mary Nichols
Hostage Bride	Anne Herries

MEDICAL

Breaking Her No-Dates Rule	Emily Forbes
Waking Up With Dr Off-Limits	Amy Andrews
Tempted by Dr Daisy	Caroline Anderson
The Fiancée He Can't Forget	Caroline Anderson
A Cotswold Christmas Bride	Joanna Neil
All She Wants For Christmas	Annie Claydon

 *Mills & Boon® Online*

Discover more romance at
www.millsandboon.co.uk

- **FREE** online reads
- **Books** up to one month before shops
- **Browse our books** before you buy

...and much more!

For exclusive competitions and instant updates:

Like us on **facebook.com/romancehq**

Follow us on **twitter.com/millsandboonuk**

Join us on **community.millsandboon.co.uk**

Visit us Online Sign up for our FREE eNewsletter at
www.millsandboon.co.uk